A Shot in the Night

Sandra Waggoner

A Shot on the Night

Printed in the United States of America First Edition: 2021

Cover Illustration: Greg & Sandra Waggoner | www.sandrawaggoner.com

With thanks, I dedicate this book to a couple of very special ladies God has blessed me to rub shoulders with. They know the Lord, and He shines in their lives.

Janet Shay: She saw a book in me and coaxed my pen to paper. She did not push or shove, but sometimes nudged a bit and blocked the gates to the wilderness!

Sheryl Garza: I thank her for her dedication to punctuation and grammar! I am in awe that her children are not named Parenthesis, Apostrophe, and Quotation Mark! ;) She sure answers all my questions about the English Language!

And thanks to my Lord who answers all my prayers…In His way, in His time, which is best for me!

"I rejoice at thy word, as one that findeth great spoil."

Psalm119:162

CONTENTS

~

A Shot in the Night

Chapter #1

Thick moisture wet and weighed down the night air. It felt like a damp quilt had been tossed over his world. He stilled his oars to listen and reached over to touch Ole Honker's nose, urging his dog to be silent. The hound understood and licked his hand. A moment ago, the bullfrogs had been having a camp meeting sing-along in competition with a gossip session on the banks. Now, the silence was deafening. Chills trekked up the boy's back. Someone on shore violently gasped for air. He and his dog were not alone. Someone was out there among the trees. Clay held his breath and listened. He shivered, not with cold, but with eerie foreboding. His boat was in the middle of the river, and that was the last place he wanted to be. Any shaft of moonlight that might filter through the fog would be a finger pointing at him.

A drop of water fell from his lifted oar and plopped into the river, shattering the silence.

On shore, a stick cracked, and a gravelly voice whispered, "I know you are out there. You might as well show yerself."

Had he been seen? His heart pounded. Clay did not even dare to breathe.

"Awe, there you are." He chuckled, "I'll get you now."

A Shot in the Night

A shot cracked through the silence of the dark night, followed by a yelp, a crash, and thrashing in the trees.

The man on shore chuckled. "Gotcha! Told you I never miss." The man took out running toward his prey.

Clay could barely make him out as he gulped in a breath of relief. The man had not been after him, and chances were he had not seen him in the fog. "Good," he whispered. Clay dipped his oars in the water and turned his boat toward the other side of the river. There was no way he wanted to be seen by that shooter, much less be caught by him.

"Girlie, you best come with me." The fog made the voice sound like a shout. "Leave that ole dead man, and I'll take good care of you."

Clay stopped his oars. There was a dead man AND a girl?

"No! Don't touch me," the girl sobbed. "I won't go anywhere with you. You shot him! You killed him! You murdered him!"

Clay heard the girl's defiant answer. Her voice shook, but it was strong.

"Jumpin' Jehoshaphat!" He mumbled and shook his head. No, he did not want to be caught by that man, but he would not leave the girl with a man who had just killed another… not if he could help it. He turned the boat and dipped the oars deep into the water. Through the thick fog, he rowed until he nosed into the shore. Then, he stealthily stepped out and tethered his boat with a loose slip knot because he would need his boat fast when he returned.

"Come on, Ole Honker. I might need your help, but you've got to be quiet," Clay whispered.

The hound tipped his head and slid his nose into the palm of Clay's hand.

Silently, Clay and his dog stepped into the trees using the big trunks for cover.

"Come on over here, Girlie," the man with the gun tried to make his voice pleasant as he coaxed the girl.

"No! Don't touch me! You killed my pa! You murderer!" She was sobbing now. "My papa didn't even have a weapon!"

"Now, Girlie, I didn't know he was your pa. I thought he was a deer. In this fog, anyone could of made a mistake like that."

"It wasn't a mistake. Pa said he watched you shooting at those men who worked on the pipeline. Pa said you didn't want us here, and it was your way of getting rid of the lot of us." Her voice rose to a shout.

The man looked around to ensure that they were alone.

Clay eased closer. He could see the shadowy figures now, and he could feel Ole Honker's urge to jump into the middle of it. He knelt beside his dog and whispered, "Not yet, Ole Honker. Not yet."

The dog sat. His hair bristled on his back.

Clay's heart raced.

The girl stood stiff with her fists balled at her sides.

The man's eyes seemed to glow in the shadows as he inched closer to the girl.

The dead man lay sprawled between them, and there was no question but that he was dead. The bullet had found its mark right between his eyes, which now stared at nothing.

The chills of fear Clay had felt before were trampled by anger. This man had killed an unarmed man, and Clay had heard him when the man had sighted in on his prey. "Gotcha! Told you I never miss!" Could he have been talking to a deer? Every ounce of his being shouted, "No." Besides, at this distance, this man would know a man from a deer even in the fog. He knew who he was shooting at, and he had intended to kill his prey. Even now, as the man spoke to the girl, his voice was tainted with the celebration of victory.

The man inched closer to the girl until the only thing between them was her dead Pa.

As Clay watched, the man sought to step over the dead body and grab the girl. He tripped on the leg of the girl's Pa and smashed to his knees. Wildly, the girl kicked, hitting the man in the chin with her boot. He crashed backward over the body, yelling not-so-nice words. The jolt made the dead man's arm flop over the shooter's neck. In terror, the shooter clawed at the dead arm, yelling, "No! No! He's got me! The Devil's come for me!" The two men, one alive and the other dead, seemed to roll and shriek together on the ground.

Even the forest shuttered to a standstill.

The girl jolted into action. Her skirts flew as she blindly ran through the trees right at Clay.

The boy grabbed the girl.

She gasped and yanked in a gulp of air to scream.

Clay smothered his hand over her mouth and hissed, "I'm on your side. Let's get out of here." He slowly eased his hand from her lips.

Her eyes sparked, "I won't leave my pa here with that horrible man, that…that monster, that horrible Beast."

He grabbed her shoulders and looked into her eyes. "That man cannot kill your pa again, but he can kill you and me, or worse. Our best chance is to get out while he is still fighting with…" He let the sentence hang. How could he describe the fight with a deranged killer and a dead man that would probably end any minute now? He shrugged. "That man will be antsy when he comes to his senses… if he has any senses left. We need to be gone by then."

"And where do you plan on going?"

"Town. We need to get the Sheriff."

Violently, she shook her head. "We can't get the Sheriff."

"Why not?"

"Do you know who that man is?" She pointed over her shoulder at the man trying to escape the grips of the dead.

Clay narrowed his eyes, "No. I've heard the voice before, but it's dark. I can't place him."

With both hands, she swiped at the tears still streaming down her face. "I can place him. I know him. That man is Deputy Irwin Sneedle."

Clay gasped. "The deputy? Are you sure?"

"You bet, I am sure. Deputy Irwin Sneedle. He has been to our home many times, and he is not a nice man." She turned and spat on the ground.

Clay clasped his hands behind his head and looked to the sky. This was good to know. "Then we won't be going to the sheriff. But we still need to get out of here. We can't do a thing for your pa, and I am sure your pa would want me to get you safe home."

"But…"

The hound dog whined.

The boy grabbed her arm. "Listen. Ole Honker hears that man coming."

The girl looked over her shoulder, grabbed his hand, and nodded.

"Good. Let's go. He already knows we are here, so let's run."

The two, trailed by Ole Honker, ran. Branches grabbed at them, and roots tripped them, causing them to stumble. Spanish moss wrapped its moist, hairy fingers through their hair and about their necks. At the boat, Clay grabbed the girl, waded through the water, and sat her on the boat's one bench seat. He pulled the ground rope and hopped in.

The man, Deputy Irwin Sneedle, burst into the clearing with a stumbling run. His shirt was ripped to shreds, and his hat was gone. "Get out of that boat now! You are under arrest. I'm taking you in!" His voice shook as he shouted through the fog.

Ole Honker lunged from the reeds in the shallow water with a howl that echoed for miles.

The man threw his hands wide, then struggled to get a hold of himself.

Clay grabbed his oars and sank them deep into the water.

Deputy Sneedle threw his hands up desperately, trying to balance himself so he could aim his rifle.

The hound dove and hit the man in the chest, knocking him to the ground. The dog wrapped his teeth about Deputy Sneedle's neck and growled.

Deputy Sneedle tried to slug the dog, but one arm was pinned beneath him, and the other was tangled between his rifle and the monster dog. "Call off your dog, or I'll kill him!" he ground through clenched teeth.

Ole Honker growled back and clamped his jaws a bit tighter.

Deputy Sneedle coughed. He could not get his breath.

From the boat, Clay watched. "I should let Ole Honker have him," he breathed, "but it would probably poison my dog, and he's a good dog, maybe the best there is." He whistled to Ole Honker.

Ole Honker paused, but the dog did not let go of his hold on the man's neck.

The girl had her arms wrapped around her, and she was shuddering. Her pa was dead, her heart was broken, but her eyes shot sparks. "I wish I could kill him."

Clay nodded, "But then you would have to live with it the rest of your life."

"I could."

"You might, but wouldn't you rather see him hang?" He winked at the girl. Again, Clay whistled to Ole Honker. "Good job, Boy. Leave him to rot."

Ole Honker growled in warning as he loosened his jaws.

The man struggled to sit but slouched back into the mud, coughing and choking.

Ole Honker turned and pranced toward the water. At the edge, he leaped through the air and sailed into the boat.

"I'll find you," the gravelly voice threatened as it ended in a coughing spree.

The dog whined, inching closer to the girl.

Clay smiled. "She's okay, Boy. Take good care of her."

Ole Honker slunk beside the girl, sat, and lay his head in her lap.

The girl slid off the bench to the floor of the boat and wrapped her arms around the dog's neck. Then she cried.

Clay sat on the bench and took the oars, digging them deep into the water. The boat swung into the current and set them midstream.

Behind them, the angry man pulled himself to his feet. He grabbed his rifle, aimed, and shot. His aim was shaky due to wrestling with the dead man and then that monster dog. He dropped the gun to his side and yelled, "I will find out who you are, and I will take care of you!"

The boat disappeared into the fog.

A Shot in the Night

Night on the River

Chapter #2

A shaft of moonlight sliced through the fog, singling out the girl with Clay's dog sitting together in front of him. They looked like they were getting along pretty well. She still had her arm around Ole Honker, and every now and again, the dog's gray-blue eyes found her chocolate browns still swimming in tears. The dog whined and scooted closer. Clay sighed. He may have lost his dog to this girl.

The night seemed calm, as if all terror…like ice cream had been scooped and gulped away, and the last crunchy bite of the cone had been swallowed. Only the quiet of sweet memory was left. But this memory was not sweet. It was one seared into the heart as a brand. It would last forever.

Clay looked at the girl. He needed to find out where to take her. How? "Ole Honker likes you a lot."

She nodded. "I like him a lot."

He swung the oars a few more times before he asked. "Could you tell me your name?"

She hesitated. "Bee Poppy. My granny tells me that my mom always loved bees and bright red poppies. She would sit and watch bees all afternoon if she could. And poppies? Granny said she would press them between paper, let them dry, and draw them into dancing fairies with bright red dresses."

"You have any of those drawings?" Clay asked.

"No," she looked across the river at nothing.

"You should ask her."

The girl shook her head. "She comes and goes, and she goes a bunch more than she comes. My granny and papa are who I live with…well, until now." She paused and whispered, "Papa is dead."

Clay whistled. "I am sorry. Your papa and now your pa! That is a hard break."

Bee Poppy looked over the water. "That was my papa back there. He's the one Deputy Sneedle murdered."

"But I thought you called him 'Pa' out there along the river?" Clay asked.

A quiet giggle slipped over her lips. "I did. Ever since I started talking, they have told me I called him Papa. Sometimes, I shorten it to Pa."

Clay nodded in the dark. "Mmm, Bee Poppy," he paused. "That is a mouthful of a name."

The girl smiled, "So? Change it. I really don't care."

The boy grinned. "You don't care?" He looked across the water, smiled, and laughed. "Beep."

"Beep?" she furrowed her brow. "Why Beep?"

"Because. Because you make noise. You don't back down. It's like the squeaky horn on those automobiles. They got to let everyone know they are taking over the road."

Bee Poppy squeezed the hound dog's neck. "I like that name, Ole Honker. I like that name. Beep. Ain't nobody got that name but me."

The silence on the water was deafening. Clay broke it with a question. "Where do I need to take you, Beep?"

She swallowed, "I have got to tell my granny. She was afraid something like this would happen. She begged Papa to stay home. She said she had the heebie-jeebies about his going out on the river tonight. But Papa told her he had to go. He thought he knew where things were happening." Beep hugged Ole Honker's neck and sighed. "I guess he knew all right. I think Granny knew, too."

Only the oars dipping and pulling water talked.

Finally, Clay asked, "Was that true, what you said about Deputy Sneedle shooting at pipeline workers?"

The girl squinted her eyes and studied the boy before she answered. "You were there tonight. You were close enough to see what happened. My papa is," she paused and corrected herself, "My papa was a pipeline worker. Now my papa is dead, and there is no way on this earth I will ever believe Deputy Sneedle thought he was a deer." She spat into the water.

Clay took a deep breath. He nodded. He had thought the same thing. Deputy Sneedle knew what he was doing and who he was shooting. He just didn't know he had been seen.

The girl absently toyed with Ole Honker's floppy ears as she stared over the water at nothing. A shaft of moonlight broke through the fog and gleamed on the streaks where her tears had flowed.

Clay swallowed. "Do you think Deputy Sneedle was going to kill you? You're only a kid girl."

She narrowed her eyes and looked him up and down before she answered. "Let me tell you this, Deputy Sneedle don't care if I am only a kid girl like you say, which I am not." She pointed to her chest and declared, "I am thirteen, almost a woman!"

Clay raised his eyebrows, but he didn't say a word.

The girl gritted her teeth. "And for your information, Deputy Sneedle will have to kill me because there is no way I am going to keep my papa's death quiet. I will tell everyone in Rocky Branch," she paused, "Not just in Rocky Branch, but in the whole world. I will tell exactly what Deputy Sneedle did to my papa, and I will tell them I saw it all!"

"What if they turn a blind eye to it?"

She shrugged. "You mean, what if they don't believe me?"

"Yeah," Clay nodded.

"Oh, they will believe me. But this is Rocky Branch, and their problem is they do not want to think their precious deputy is a cold-blooded killer."

Clay sighed. He knew who would win this battle. The people did not want the pipeline workers around. They wanted the pipeline but not the workers. They thought the workers sullied their town. "Beep, what will you do if they choose not to believe you?"

She nibbled on her bottom lip before she answered. "Really, it would not surprise me if they don't believe me. They don't like us pipeline workers, but killing the lot of us is not going to get that pipeline done. None of the people here want to work on it, especially since pipeline workers keep disappearing." She narrowed her eyes, "My papa made number seven." She choked on the last word and whispered again, "Number seven."

Silence spread thick over the water.

"You know of seven pipeline workers who have been killed? Can you name them?"

Beep nodded. "You bet I can. My papa and I were keeping a list just like private detectives." She closed her eyes, took a deep breath, and began naming the missing. "The first one missing was Charlie Walker. She held up her pointing finger. She continued holding a finger in tribute to each missing man. Then Martin Dowling, next Henry Baker, after him, was Beuford Hicks, then Max Crowning, then Donald Mason, and now, this very night, my papa, George Washington Johnston." She counted her raised fingers. "One, two, three, four, five, six, seven. Seven good men. And all of them were killed by trash!" The girl sobbed.

Tears she didn't want poured down her cheeks. She took the hem of her dress and whipped them away. She swallowed.

It was a long time before either broke the silence. The dip of the oars and an occasional croak of a bold bullfrog seemed the only muffled sounds left of this horrible night.

Quietly, Clay spoke, "You can make the count eight." He paused and looked beyond the fog before he finished. "My dad has been missing for a whole week now."

Beep gasped. "Your dad? He worked for the pipeline?"

Clay nodded. "Sort of." The boy didn't feel like saying anything more. He did not think he could talk around the lump in his throat.

Ole Honker whined.

Beep couldn't take her gaze from the boy who had rescued her. With her brown eyes swimming, she spoke, "I'm sorry. I didn't think. I didn't know. I don't even know your name."

The boy steadied his eyes somewhere far over the river. "Clay." He dipped his oars in the water and pulled heavy strokes. They would row close to Rocky Branch before long, and he still didn't know where to take the girl.

Beep asked, "Is that why you were out there on the river tonight? Were you looking for your dad?"

Clay nodded. "Been going out every night since he's been gone."

Beep nodded. "I am truly sorry." She paused, "And…I do think you saved my life tonight. I'm glad you were out on the water. Thank you."

The boy nodded. The silence was heavy and long. Clay had been afraid to think his dad might be dead. Now, that seemed the only thing left to think. His heart dropped into his stomach, and he hoped he wouldn't be sick.

Beep stared at him. Her eyes fell to waver over the river. They would be close to Rocky Branch before long. She took deep breaths before she spoke her thoughts out loud, "How will I ever tell Granny?"

Clay shrugged. "How do I get you to your granny's?"

"Pull to the right bank before we get into Rocky Branch." She emphasized the word 'before' with her finger. Our cabin is behind the Best Biscuits Around Café. But I don't want anyone to see me. I don't want anyone to know I was gone."

Clay nodded. He preferred that no one knew he had been gone, either. "Your granny, the cook at the cafe?"

"Of course, it's the Best Biscuits Around Café," she smiled. "You come with me, and I know she'll give you a biscuit and maybe some jam piled on it. She is the best cook Rocky Branch has ever had."

A smile tickled his lips as they pulled up to the bank. He stepped out of his boat and tethered it to a post.

Beep stood. The boat rocked.

Clay grabbed her hand to steady the girl as she turned to step ashore.

Ole Honker's tongue hanging out flapped as he jumped to the bank.

Stealthily, they edged into the trees as they snuck into Rocky Branch and finally to the back of the café, across the alleyway, and behind the cabin into the breezeway. Beep lightly touched the door. The hinges whined, and the door swung open. Her breath caught. Her eyes flashed a warning to Clay. She whispered, "Granny has never left the breezeway door unlocked at night, much less unlatched. Something must be wrong." Her heart raced, and chills crawled up her arms. She stepped inside and searched the darkness of the cabin one more time. She stifled a scream, turned to run back outside, and smacked into Clay. They tumbled over Ole Honker, landing in a pile on the breezeway boards. Ole Honker howled. The dog tore into the cabin and ran out the alley door, chasing some man.

"Granny!" Beep whisper-shouted. She scrambled to her feet, raced into the cabin, and stopped dead in her tracks.

Granny couldn't answer. She was stretched across the floor.

Beep stumbled and dropped to her side, "Granny?" Beep shook her arm and pleaded, "Granny, Granny, oh Granny! Please wake up."

Granny didn't move, and Beep wasn't sure she was even breathing.

A Shot in the Night

Best Biscuits Around Café

Chapter #3

Clay jumped to his feet and sprang into the cabin. It only took a minute to know he couldn't help here, but he could chase the man flying down the alley. There was a shot and a yelp. "Oh, No! Ole Honker!" Clay yelled as he blasted through the yawning alley door and into the alleyway behind The Best Biscuits Around Café. Ole Honker raced back to the cabin and through the open door. The hound did not seem to be hurt as he landed at Beep's side, and Clay knew his dog, his friend, would be fine. But the intruder from Beep's cabin was getting away. Clay watched the man disappear around the corner of The Best Biscuits Around Café. The boy barreled after him. At the corner of the alley, Clay slowed and leaned against the back of the building. It would not be wise to follow the man into the side alley. He might be waiting for him to do that very thing. Clay squatted and edged his head around the corner of the building to see where the man had gone. He saw nothing, yet that did not mean the man was not lurking behind one of the many rusty trash barrels. Again, Clay plastered himself against the rock wall. He took a deep breath and decided what he would do. Lightly, he sped back along the wall and stopped at the rear door of the café. He reached out and tried the handle. Locked. He slid by the door and to the window beside it, which was opened a crack. Gently, he raised the window, slipped his leg over the windowsill, and stepped into the dark room. The crowd of empty tables and chairs was shadowy quiet, and he had to inch slowly through them to the front of the café. A streetlamp lit the big front store window enough that Clay watched the black silhouette of Granny's attacker crouching with a gun, pointing at the entrance to the side alley, which he expected Clay to run through at any moment.

Clay smiled. His dad had raised no fool. Softly, the boy crept to the door. He hoped the hinges were well-oiled. He didn't have a gun, but that man lurking out there waiting for him didn't know he had no gun. His eyes traveled about him until they landed on what he wanted: a broom. It would work. He looked above the door before he opened it and smiled. Just as he thought. A bell hung there to jingle when customers came in. Clay stood on his tiptoes, took his knife, and slashed through the string. Then he shoved the bell deep into his pants pocket.

So very gently, he opened the door. He stepped out and prayed the boardwalk would not creak. Two quiet steps… Clay shoved the handle of the broom into the back of the crouching man.

Clay deepened his voice as much as he could. "You breathe a breath, and I'll shoot your guts clear to Farmerville. And that's a long way."

The man froze.

"Drop the gun and raise your hands high," Clay ordered.

The man dropped the gun and raised his hands.

"Now, toss your gun into the street."

The man tossed his gun.

It was then that two things happened. A man staggered out of The Branch Water Brewing Company singing, "God bless America…" and Ole Honker exploded upon the boardwalk, snarling at Clay's captive. Terrified, the prisoner jumped, dived into the alley, and blasted into its darkness.

Clay dropped from the boardwalk, grabbed the gun his prisoner had thrown in the street, aimed, and fired at the fleeing man. He couldn't see, yet he knew he had missed the running figure because the man yelped and charge down the alley even faster than before.

But Ole Honker ran after him, and the chase was on!

The man and Ole Honker were gone. Somewhere, they were still running, and Clay knew Ole Honker was going to get even with the enemy.

Clay sighed. He tucked the gun in the back of his waistband and beneath his jacket. He grabbed the broom just as men flooded the street from The Branch Water Brewing Company.

"Hey, you there, Boy," a big man pointed and headed Clay's way. "Did you see what happened out here?"

Clay shook his head. "No." he lied. "I was just finishing. The Lady said she would give me biscuits and gravy in the morning if I swept the place. I had just blown the last lights out when I heard some ruckus out front, so I came to see what was happening. What did you guys see?"

"We didn't see a thing, but we sure heard a gunshot!" They huddled close together.

"I heard a gunshot, too," Clay agreed.

The man who had been singing was leaning over a hitching rail, puking. No one bothered to ask him anything.

"Men," someone was taking charge. "Men, I think someone ran down this alley. Let's go check it out."

The tight group of men followed their leader.

Clay let out a slow breath. He took the broom and swept off the boards where mud from the alley had been tracked from his captive's boots. Quietly, he opened the front door to The Best Biscuits Around Café, stepped inside, and closed the door, and locked it. He stood the broom where he had found it and tiptoed to the back door. He looked both ways before stepping out to ensure the posse of men from The Branch Water Brewing Company could not be seen. He was in luck. They were all out of sight, but he could still hear them arguing about which way to go next.

At the open door of Beep's Cabin, Clay tapped. He didn't want to frighten the girl. She had already been through so much tonight.

"Yes?" she whispered.

"Your granny? How is she doing?" Clay asked, praying he was right and that she was alive.

Beep sat back on the floor beside her granny and rubbed her temples, "I was hoping you would come back. Granny is alive, but she is not too clear about what happened. She said she heard someone at the breezeway door and thought it was Papa and me. She got out of her rocker to open the door for us, and that man pushed her, and she fell over her chair. She said that she either hit her head on something when she fell, or he hit her on the head after she fell. She didn't know for sure which."

"You think she will be fine?"

Beep shrugged. "I hope so. She's healthy and very stubborn."

Clay murmured, "Good. She'll need to be stubborn."

"Clay, I need help getting her up and into bed. Would you?"

He smiled. "Sure thing." He paused and gently took her hand, pulling her up beside him. Then he turned her to face him and whispered, "Did you tell her about your papa?"

She violently shook her head. "Promise me you won't say a word!" she hissed, her eyes wild with fire.

Clay took a step back. "Promise, cross my," he crossed his heart, "and hope to die." He took his forefinger and sliced it across his throat.

"Good." She nodded. "And don't think I won't help you die if you breathe a word."

"What are you two in cahoots about, all whispering like in the dark?" Granny furrowed her eyebrows together. "You best light a lamp and fix to getting me offin' this cold floor."

"Yes, ma'am," Clay was the first to answer.

Granny narrowed her eyes and studied the boy while Beep lit a lamp.

"A young man? Bee Poppy, what you doin' with a young man? You knows you're way too young to be fiddling with any young man." Granny sat up all by herself.

Clay's eyes widened, and he tipped his head in question at Beep.

Granny grabbed the edge of the table and pulled herself up slowly to stand. "I ain't hurt enough that I can't take care of things like young men comin' a-callin' a girl way too young to be called upon."

"Granny!" Beep was embarrassed. "It is not like that. Clay didn't come calling. I…I…well…I got separated from Papa, and Clay found me and…and…Clay brought me home."

Granny didn't say a word, but her eyes traveled up, down, and all over Clay.

Clay wanted to hide more than the uncomfortable gun in the waistband of his trousers.

"Step up here, young man, and let me take a closer look at ya," Granny left no room for argument.

Clay glanced at Beep.

Beep nodded.

Clay stepped a bit closer.

Granny stirred her finger in a circle. "Turn around, young man."

Clay stood straighter than ever and turned a full circle.

"Humph, guess he don't look to be too much older than your own self, Bee Poppy. But," she looked at Clay with her eyebrows lowered, "you don't touch her, young man."

Clay swallowed, "Yes, Ma'am."

"And," Granny continued, "Miss Bee Poppy, you don't touch him neither!"

"Granny!" Beep gasped.

"You both understand?" Granny put a hand over her heart.

In unison, both Beep and Clay said, "Yes, Ma'am."

Clay felt like saluting the lady, but he also felt that if he did, he might be thrown into the brig and never let out.

"Good." Granny raised her eyes to heaven and said, "Dear Lord, watch over these two children because I am limited in my sight. I can't be everywhere all the time like you can, Lord, so I am leaving them in your hands. Amen."

Clay had dropped his head the minute Granny had said, 'Dear Lord,' and now he was afraid to look up at her, 'Amen.'

Beep nudged him with her foot, and his head popped up. He hoped Granny hadn't noticed Beep's nudge. She might take that as touching.

"Good," Granny began.

Clay felt like thanking the Lord that Granny hadn't noticed.

"Now," Granny continued, "I feel a bit shaky, so I am going to sit in my rocker. Bee Poppy, I would like a hot cup of tea, and, Young Man, I would like a cold rag for the back of my neck."

Beep pressed her lips together and smiled at her granny. "Granny, the young man's name is Clay, and Granny, I know you know how to say please because you have taught me to always use that word."

Granny laughed, "So I have, so I have. Bee Poppy, would you please fix me a hot cup of tea …and…" she winked at Clay!

Clay's mouth dropped open.

Granny chuckled. "Clay, would you be so kind as to fetch me a cool rag for the back of my neck? Please?"

Clay looked from Granny to Beep and back again before he answered, "Yes, Ma'am."

Clay grabbed the bucket to get water, opened the door, and Ole Honker pranced proudly through the door, displaying a chunk of plaid pants material swaying from his mouth.

Clay laughed. He and his dog both had a chunk of the enemy. "Good Boy, Ole Honker! Good Boy!" He reached down to scruff Ole Honker and felt something wet. He knelt beside his dog. Clay picked up his floppy ear and shook his head. "Looks like you got your ear pierced, Ole Boy. We'll have to clean you up and find a fancy earring to hang in that bullet hole." Clay chuckled, swallowed, and hugged his dog. "I'm sure glad that bullet wasn't a might closer to your head."

Ole Honker whined.

Biscuits and Jelly

Chapter #4

It had been a short night, and morning found Clay lying on the bench across the street from The Best Biscuits Around Café with Ole Honker at his feet. He yawned, sat up, and tipped his hat back on his head. After the ruckus, which had emptied most of the Branch men to search the streets, Rocky Branch had settled to a quiet night. Clay had slept soundly with Ole Honker keeping watch under his bench. Clay stretched. He rubbed his backbone, especially his waist. He wasn't used to the gun he had tucked inside his waistband next to his backbone. Ole Honker stood with his forelegs pushed out in front of him and did the same wake-up stretching. He spread his mouth wide, squeaking as if his jaws needed to be oiled. His dangling tongue danced a jig hanging from the side of his mouth.

Pink sun rays, as fingers stretched over the sky, poking sleep from the dark corners of the day. Clay smiled as the aroma of biscuits enticed his tummy. He stood to stretch the kinks from his arms and legs. The lamp in the kitchen must have been lit before the sun had peeked over the eastern horizon. He sat back down. The bench was hard, and the waiting was even harder. He had thought of so many things he needed to ask Beep, but they had agreed. He was to stay across the street until she stepped out of the front door to shake and lay the welcome rug in place. Most importantly, Clay wondered whether Beep had told her granny about her papa's death, and whether she had told the whole truth about all that had happened last night. Somehow, he was going to have to get Beep alone so they could get their stories straight.

A crowd was gathering in front of the café, but Beep had not brought out the welcome mat yet. Clay rubbed his hands up and down his pant legs. He was hungry, and he needed to talk to Beep. He looked at the gathering. Some he recognized, and some he didn't. There were enough people that he could no longer see them all. In fact, he couldn't see if Beep had slipped out the door to lay out the welcome mat.

Finally, the door opened, and the crowd poured into the café. Clay took a deep, hungry breath. He had thought it smelled good when the door was closed, but now the sweet aroma tantalized him. His tummy was in rebellion with his body challenging Ole Honker's fiercest warning growls. He had no money to buy breakfast, but Beep had promised biscuits with jelly and maybe gravy.

There was no welcome mat. "Wonder why?" he asked Ole Honker.

The dog wagged his tail.

Clay reached down and patted Ole Honker. "Beep told me to wait until I saw her put out the welcome mat, and I haven't seen her yet. And… no mat either."

Now, the crowd was inside. He stood to get a better view, but he still saw no welcome mat in front of the door, so he had not missed that. Beep told him to watch for her and the mat. Had she forgotten? Maybe her granny had changed her plans.

Clay paced to the edge of the boardwalk and leaned against the porch pole. He sighed and turned back to the bench. He would wait a bit longer. He sat up straight on the bench. He tried to see through the big front window, but he couldn't make out who the shapes inside the café were.

"Boy," a big man in need of a shave with a bowler hat had quietly stepped beside him. He nudged Clay's shoulder. "Boy, there's a man in that café who wants to talk to you," he pointed at the café.

Clay looked up into the man's face and recognized him. His cheeks were still rosy from last night, and Clay thought the tune of 'God Bless America' was probably still rolling around in his head. Clay steadied his gaze on the man. "Who wants to see me?"

The man shrugged. "Don't rightly know, but he's sportin' a badge of some kind. I think it might be the sheriff. Anyway, he told me he would give me two bits for breakfast if I got you there. So, how about it? You want to get me breakfast, Boy?"

Clay watched the door. Could that be why Beep didn't put out the welcome mat? Maybe it was the sheriff, but what if it was Deputy Sneedle? Clay didn't think Deputy Sneedle knew him. Last night had been foggy and dark. Surely, the deputy wouldn't recognize him. Clay hesitated as he watched the door across the street.

"Come on, Boy. I lost all my money at the Branch last night, and I'm so hungry I think my stomach is gnawin' on my backbone. You'd be doing me a mighty fine favor."

Clay watched the door across the street. "What's he look like, the man that wants to see me?"

The man shrugged, "He's skinny, and he's wallowin' in self-pity or somethin'. He looks like he lost a battle with maybe a coyote, a porcupine, or a bobcat. He doesn't smell like a skunk, so it can't have been that. And he's sittin' at the table off in the corner of the café. He's got his hat pulled low over his eyes, and I think he's tryin' not to be noticed, but he is sure watchin' the door."

Clay shook his head. Of all the luck! The description sounded like Deputy Sneedle, and if he was, that would explain why Beep had not thrown out the welcome mat. She wouldn't want him to walk in on that Deputy Sneedle, and she sure wouldn't want the deputy to see her either.

"Boy, he said if you won't come in, he would have to find the girl on his own," the man shrugged his shoulders, "You want me to go tell him to start lookin' for the girl?"

Clay's heart skipped a beat. It had to be Deputy Sneedle, and he was looking for Beep. The deputy might not know him, but he would never forget Beep. Clay shook his head. "No. I will go talk to the man, and I guess you had better come with me to get your free breakfast."

The man smiled, "I'd be pleased."

They walked across the street together. Ole Honker whined and followed. At the door, Clay reached down and told his hound to stay. He was pretty sure Beep's Granny wouldn't welcome Ole Honker in her café.

The old dog whined, but he lay down on the boardwalk close to the door.

Clay promised, "I'll bring you something good, Ole Boy."

Clay turned to the man, "You come with me, and I want you to sit at the table with the man who told you to come get me. No matter what he says, just sit at the table. Maybe you could sit before he even has a chance to say anything. Understand?"

"Boy, I sure do." The man's stomach growled.

It was Deputy Irwin Sneedle, alright, and Clay thought the big man had made a good call. The fight Deputy Sneedle had had with the dead man and then Ole Honker had left sign all over his face. A black eye was swollen to a slit, and his cheeks were cut and bruised. One earlobe dangled by a thin thread of skin. His lips were cracked in a couple of places, and a chunk of his scroungy beard had been yanked out. He had changed clothes since last night, but it hadn't helped much.

Clay pulled out the chair across from the Deputy and sat. He motioned for his companion to do the same.

Clay studied the deputy's face again before he asked, "What's the other man look like?"

Deputy Sneedle glared. "It weren't no man, Kid."

Clay thought he hated this man. He took a slow, deliberate breath and almost whispered, "Not a man? Maybe something from the dead? I've heard of haunts. Maybe you fought with a haunt?"

An insane flicker lit Deputy Sneedle's eye. Wildly, he jumped to his feet and grabbed the boy across the table by his shirt collar, and pulled him to his nose, yelling, "It was you on the river last night, wasn't it, Kid?"

"Haunts?" The big, hungry man wanting breakfast scooted his chair away from the table and shook. He was hungry, but his appetite was fading. His eyes grew to full rounds that surely would glow in the dark if they had a chance. "For all that is holy, put the boy down, Deputy. Haunts won't like you treating a boy that way, and they'll follow you to the ends of the earth."

The deputy shuddered and dropped the kid. Clay slammed into the seat of the chair.

Clay's heart was pounding, and it felt like he had to swallow his heart to answer. "Deputy Sneedle, I don't go any place where haunts roam, so whatever you are talking about, it could not have been me."

The deputy looked at the crowd, watching his every move, and slowly sat down.

Clay swallowed as his eyes landed on Deputy Sneedle's badge. He pressed his lips together before he spoke. He knew he had the attention of everyone in the café. He spoke slowly and clearly. "Deputy Sneedle, your badge has something caked on it, and it is covering the D E in deputy. It makes your badge read 'Puty Sneedle. And…" he pushed his head closer to examine the badge. "I think those two letters are covered with blood; dried, caked blood!" He looked 'Puty Sneedle in the eye and spoke slowly so all could hear, "Maybe it's the blood of haunts?"

Everyone in the café had stopped eating to stare, and silence had settled like a shroud. Finally, a gasp broke the quiet.

Deputy Sneedle dropped his hand to his badge, yanked it from his vest, and shoved it into his pocket without looking at it. "Ain't none of your business," he hissed.

Then, the deputy became aware of the silent crowd staring at him. He looked around. Hastily, he stood scooting his chair against the back wall. He reached for his money belt, fumbled with the latch, and finally pulled out a wad of money. He threw it on the table. "There's your breakfast money, Arthur." Then he pointed and glared at Clay, "I want that girl, Kid. And I think you know exactly what I am talking about." He turned and tromped to the door.

"Don't know what you are talking about, 'Puty Sneedle," the Kid smiled.

Chuckles sifted through the café.

'Puty Sneedle burst out the door, letting it slam.

Ole Honker jumped to his feet, crouching, growling, and baring his teeth. He lunged.

Puty Sneedle looked down, yelped, and stumbled with surprise and fear. He kicked at the dog and ran down the boardwalk with his coattails flying.

Was My Dad Alive?

Chapter #5

"Well, would you believe that?" A lady gasped as she swung her loaded fork to point toward the slamming door. "That was an elected town official, wasn't it, Harold? Can you believe that? He looked awfully disgusting to be in a place of business. I wonder what happened to him?"

Across from her, her husband sat back in his chair while tapping his butter knife on his plate. "Yes, he did look under the weather, and yes, Janet, he is an elected official. Deputy Irwin Sneedle, who came highly recommended. I wonder what that was all about?"

His wife raised her eyebrows, "Well, Mr. Harold Shay, you are the mayor of this place. I think you should find out." She nodded, her blonde curls bouncing.

The mayor sighed, "I believe I will, Mrs. Mayor, but it will have to wait until after breakfast. This is too good to waste. Almost as good as your biscuits, My Dear."

"Thank you, Sweetie," she smiled.

The big, hungry man who had begged Clay for his breakfast by coaxing him into the café sat and looked up at the boy. "You might as well set a spell, Boy. It looks like Deputy Sneedle left enough money for both your breakfast and mine. I'm hungry, but

I'm plenty willing to share. Besides," he tipped his head and looked up at Clay, speaking low, "Is there something that I should know?"

Clay narrowed his eyes to study the man before he sat. Something was different. This man did not sound the same, and his face had taken on a serious look. He was not carrying the drowsy, drunken slouch he had worn before. And what did the man mean by asking if there was something he needed to know? Clay hadn't been taught to share secrets with strangers.

The man let his eyes rove about the room before he whispered, "You can trust me."

Without taking his eyes from the man, Clay sat and leaned back in his chair. The man wanted his trust? He would need more persuasion than buying him breakfast to earn his trust. Clay stared at him. "Why should I trust you? I have never seen you before," he paused, watching the man's eyes, "until last night when you were singing 'God Bless America' on the boardwalk outside of The Branch." A hint of a smile touched his lips. "And the last time I saw you, you were bent over the hitching rail, tossing your guts."

The man chuckled, "You're a bright one."

Clay noticed he did not deny singing last night or the hitching rail incident, but that did not mean the man could be trusted. "Mister, honestly, you have done nothing to earn my trust."

The man nodded. "You are right, Boy. I like a careful soul. It will keep you safe."

Beep slipped up beside their table. "Can I help you, Sirs?"

The man smiled widely, showing a perfectly white set of straight teeth. "You bet you can help me, Young Lady. The name of this place advertises that you have the best biscuits around. Is that to be trusted?" He looked at Clay as he said the word 'trusted.' "I mean, it is only the sign on the door I have to go by."

Beep nodded, "Yes, Sir. My granny makes them fresh every morning and sells the last crumbs before lunch. People come from miles around for her biscuits."

The man laughed. "Sold. I trust you. I'll have your biscuits and gravy with a side of eggs over easy, and bring the same for my friend here." He waved across the table to include Clay.

Clay looked at Beep and nodded. "I'd like some jelly, too. Please."

Beep gave a wisp of a smile, and Clay could tell she had been crying.

"I'll have those orders out as soon as possible, Gentlemen."

Clay wanted to laugh. It wasn't often he was called a gentleman. He thought about last night and thought her tears probably meant she had told Granny about her papa. His heart was heavy, and he hoped Granny was fine, but how could she be fine? How could she be in the kitchen cooking?

"I'll just take these dishes out of your way," Beep reached and grabbed the plate and cup 'Puty Sneedle had left. Then she took the damp towel hanging from her arm and swiped it across the table.

The man quickly took a bill from the wad the deputy had left and handed it to Beep. "Miss, here's a tip from 'Puty Sneedle."

Beep's eyes sparkled. Clay didn't know if it was from the large tip or from someone calling the deputy 'Puty Sneedle."

"That is a very nice tip, Sir. Do I need to bring change?" Beep asked.

The man smiled that big, toothy smile meant to melt away all fears. "No, Miss. No change. You keep it all."

"Thank you, Sir," Beep shyly grinned and turned to catch Clay's eye with a bit of a nod.

Across the table, the man watched Beep disappear through the swinging door of the kitchen.

Clay couldn't figure out this man. Maybe it was the man himself. Clay did not want to like him, but he liked what he had done for Beep.

The man dropped his gaze to focus on Clay.

Clay thought he did not like that either. He did not trust this man. He had pretended to be something he was not, and yet, what he had just done for Beep was nice. Should he trust him?

The man pulled his eyes from Clay to survey the people in the restaurant again. All seemed settled and busy with their breakfasts. He reached into his inside coat pocket and slipped something out. He stretched his fist across the table and laid 'the something' wrapped in oil paper before Clay.

Slowly, Clay picked up the lump and unfolded the paper, unwrapping what was inside. Clay sucked in a breath, yanking his heart to a standstill. It was a gold pocket watch with a gold chain. Fastened to the other end of the chain was a carved, wooden cowboy boot. Clay would know it anywhere, anytime. The watch was his dad's. His dad's Papa had carved that boot years ago and had fixed it to the other end of the gold chain. The watch, chain, and boot had been passed down from generation to generation. Clay swallowed, scooped it up, and looked the man in the eye. "How did you get this?"

"Your dad gave it to me to give to you."

Clay's appetite disappeared. His breath was gone. He couldn't talk around the lump in his throat. He closed his eyes, hoping tears didn't squeeze out. He swiped his hand across his nose. Finally, he was able to whisper, "Was my dad alive?"

The man put his elbows on the table, clasped his hands together, and rested his chin on them. "I won't lie to you, Boy. He was alive when I left him, but it didn't look good for him."

"You left him in bad shape? Where?" Clay gasped and jumped from the chair.

"Sit down. People are looking at you."

The boy swept the café with his eyes. Everyone had stopped eating to look at him. Slowly, he swallowed and sat. "Why did you leave him if he was in bad shape?" Although he whispered, he knew he was glaring at the man, and he didn't care.

"I had to, Boy. Your dad wouldn't have it any other way. He told me it would be too dangerous for me and too dangerous for you. And he insisted this, he tapped Clay's fist holding the watch, was too important. He had to get his message into the right hands." The man took his bowler hat off and whipped it against his leg. Then he ran his fingers through his dark, curly hair. "I did not have a choice. They were coming, and he did not want me to be caught. Boy, I left him because he wanted to keep you safe. He made me promise to deliver the message and to take care of you, to protect you."

"Protect me? From who?" Clay demanded.

The man shook his head. "I don't know. Your dad did not get a chance to tell me. We weren't together for very long, and I was busy tending to his wounds. He had been badly beaten, and how he got away from them, I cannot guess, but he did. In fact, most of the time I worked on him, he was unconscious."

"Where is he now? I'll go get him," Clay hissed from across the table.

"Safe, I hope by now. Which means I have no clue as to where he is. But I pray he is in good hands."

"Good hands." Clay's face was set. "For your sake, I hope he is in good hands."

"The best. But it is up to the good Lord if he makes it," the man looked directly into his eyes.

"Who are you anyway?" Clay asked.

The man paused. "Arthur Kent."

Clay tipped his head to the side, "But that is not your real name, is it?"

The man narrowed his eyes. "Why not?"

Clay took the paper that had wrapped his dad's pocket watch. He laid it on the table and smoothed it, ironing out the wrinkles. Then he pointed to the name. "That doesn't say Arthur Kent."

The man pressed his lips into a tight line. "It's the name I go by now. For your sake and your father's sake, we will leave my name as Arthur Kent. Now, give me that paper."

"Sure, I can give you the paper, but the name," he tapped the name on the paper with his forefinger, "the name on this paper is burnt in my memory forever. So don't think you can get away with anything."

The man gave him a look for a look. "I would advise you to forget that name. It would be in your dad's and your best interests. And you must trust that I am a friend of your dad's, so I am your friend, too."

"Trust you? How? How do I know if you are a friend? You left my dad on his own to live or die. You could be the enemy. You could have been the one who beat him. So why would I trust you?"

Beep slipped behind the man to slide a plate of steaming biscuits with gravy and eggs in place. "There you go, Sir." With a quick wink for Clay, she promised, "I'll be right back with your order plus a side of homemade jelly."

Clay softened, "Thanks, and could we get some coffee?"

"Coffee for both of you?" she asked.

Clay gave a nod. "Yes. I've been drinking coffee since I was weaned."

The girl laughed. "I'll be right back with your plate and your coffee, Sir." She raised her eyebrows and tipped her head.

Clay watched her walk away.

"You don't know that you can trust me. I understand. I am asking you to trust me. Your dad trusted me. One thing you do know is that I am not a friend of Deputy Sneedle. Does that help?"

"Maybe." He swallowed and looked directly into Arthur Kent's eyes, "Can you tell me if Deputy Sneedle is a part of them, the enemy that wants my dad dead?" Clay asked.

Arthur Kent dropped his eyes for a whisp of a second. "I don't know."

Clay leaned forward in his chair. "But you suspect he is, don't you?"

The man nodded. "I suspect he is, but I don't think he even has a clue as to what he is a part of. I think he is being used."

"Used for what? Used by who?"

The man shook his head, "I don't know those answers… yet."

"What about the message my dad asked you to send? What was that message about?" Clay asked. "With that message, we could figure it out."

"Boy, I don't know. The message was coded, and I sent it the minute I arrived in Monroe. From there, I came here to find you. Those were your dad's orders...and your dad holds a lot of lives in his hands. I trust him. Your dad was always an honest, sincere man. I did what he told me to do."

"Was?" Clay shrank back in his chair. He put his hands over his eyes and tilted his head back. "Was?"

Trust Snuck In

Chapter #6

Arthur Kent finally won Clay over. He told of times he and Clay's dad had been stationed together during World War I before Clay was born. Clay's dad had shared some of those same stories with him.

"Mr. Kent," Clay stumbled over the fake name, but they were still in the café. Anyone who heard their conversation must know him as Mr. Kent.

Mr. Kent put down his fork on the plate that had been sopped clean with the last of his biscuits. He leaned back in his chair, satisfied. "Been a few days since I sat at a table, and I would have to agree with the name of this place."

"Best Biscuits Around Café?" Beep had walked up behind Mr. Kent.

The man was startled, but he laughed. "You have a quiet walk, Young Lady. And, yes, those biscuits, that gravy, and those eggs are the best. Are you the cook?"

Beep shook her head. "My granny. She says she has been cooking for so long that she could do it with her eyes closed. I told her I didn't think it was a good idea. We might end up with jelly in the gravy and Biscuits on top of eggs."

Mr. Kent laughed. "I think I would still eat everything on the plate."

Beep smiled, “I’ll be sure to tell my granny. She’ll like that.” She picked up his empty plate and moved to Clay’s side to stack his plate atop the one she had gathered. “More coffee?”

Mr. Kent lounged back in his chair, “Yes, Ma’am. Another cup for the road would be welcomed.”

She looked to Clay, “And you?”

Clay nodded, “Sounds good.”

When Beep set the coffee down, Mr. Kent reached over to touch her hand. “Can I pay for our breakfasts now?”

“Of course, but Clay’s breakfast is on the house, my Granny’s orders.” She lightly smiled.

Mr. Kent took the whole wad of money and handed it to Beep. “That breakfast was the best, and you keep the change, Young Lady.”

Beep’s eyes grew wide. “But this is way more than we charge for breakfast.”

“There were two of us hungry men. That makes double the work for you,” Mr. Kent tipped his head. “Plus, that breakfast was worth every penny.”

“I can bring change,” the girl told him.

“No, ma’am. I want you to keep the extra for a tip.” He smiled his healthy, toothy smile.

“Thank you,” she told him, ducking to hide the gathering of tears.

When she was gone, Clay looked at Mr. Kent. He seemed like a nice man, and maybe he should trust him. Trust was a funny word. His dad used it a lot in his sermons. He related it to faith. Clay could hear him saying, "Now faith is the substance of things hoped for, the evidence of things not seen." Then, he would go on to explain that faith is something you cannot see, but it is the solid foundation of your belief. Faith should be the black-and-white rules you live by." Clay shook his head to clear his thoughts. He did not understand building on a foundation that you cannot see. How solid could that be?

As if Mr. Kent had listened to his thoughts, he asked, "Boy, is your dad still roaming all over this country preaching the Word of the Lord?"

"Yes, Sir," He paused. "He was, and I pray he will continue. He's called a circuit-riding preacher. We came here about three months ago. Dad said God was calling him because of a need these people had." Clay took a second in thought, "Somehow, I think it was more than a need to know the Lord."

"Why?" Mr. Kent leaned in and spoke in a low voice.

Clay shrugged. "A couple of times, we have had visitors in the night. There would be a tap on the side window close to where Dad slept. Dad would slip out of his bunk quiet-like and out the door. He would be gone for a couple of hours, sneak back in, and crawl into bed. When morning came, Dad would roll over and stretch as if he had been asleep all night."

"Did you ever ask him about where he had been?"

"Once. He told me he had gone to the privy."

"Did you question him on why it took so long?"

Clay looked at the man. "That is my dad. The privy is his business. Besides, I learned a long time ago that when a subject is final, there will be no more questions."

"So, you left it at that?"

Clay grinned. "If you mean, did I ask questions about it anymore? No, I did not. But I did slip out of bed and watch where he went."

"What did you find out?"

"He didn't go to the privy. He met a man, and they talked for a while, then went off together."

"Did you hear what they said?" Mr. Kent had his arms crossed on the table now, and he was leaning toward the boy.

Clay's eyes were big. "I couldn't get that close. If my dad had found me, I would be pushing up daisies."

Mr. Kent chuckled. "Still the same ole D'Gregory. Did you get close enough to recognize the man he met with?"

"No. He had a hat pulled down to cover his face and a coat with the collar turned up around his neck, and it hung clear down to his boots. I don't think he wanted anyone to recognize him. Plus, we have only been here a few months, so I probably wouldn't have known him anyway. What I do know is that he is a couple of inches shorter than my dad and a couple of inches wider, but that could be due to the bulk of the coat. So, I have been looking for someone of the same size and build as that man."

"That's good. Any leads?"

Clay shook his head. "None. I'm still on the lookout, though."

"Good. Always keep those eyes peeled," Mr. Kent told him.

"You sound like my dad. He's told me to 'keep 'em peeled' all my born days." Clay felt sadness rolling in like dark clouds. What if he never saw his dad again?

Mr. Kent chuckled. "Yep. That's where I learned 'keep 'em peeled' from. He'd always say, "Keep 'em peeled, boys, keep 'em peeled.' Made me almost afraid to close them at night."

Clay grinned, "I know." He gazed at the man across the table. He believed he was his dad's friend. He believed he had come to help, and somehow, trust had snuck in. It was just like building a foundation on faith in what you cannot see.

"Tell me about Rocky Branch," Mr. Kent said.

"When we got here, we found an old cabin to light and sit in just outside Rocky Branch if you are headed south. After we settled into the cabin, Dad went in search of a meeting place for services. Guess where Dad found it?"

Mr. Kent shrugged.

Clay chuckled. "The Branch Water Brewing Company. The owner, Mr. Perry, said they weren't using the building on Sundays and that he'd be glad to let us use it. He did warn us to stay away from the bar because he didn't have a way to lock things up. My dad told him he was welcome to come Sundays to keep 'em eyes peeled' on things to make sure no one bothered his bar."

Mr. Kent laughed and asked, "Has Mr. Perry been coming?"

Clay grinned, "He did the first Sunday, well, for a little bit. But the first time my dad mentioned hell fire and brimstone, he tipped his hat and snuck out the back way. I guess he decided he had his own fire and brimstone in those bottles behind his counter, and the people coming would not be interested in stealing any fire and brimstone before the appointed time." His eyes twinkled, "At least, that is what my dad said."

Mr. Kent laughed, "I understand. It took me a while to get used to your dad, especially when he preached on hell fire and brimstone. I had an extra dose, though. Your dad did not preach on Sundays only. We lived together in that platoon. He took advantage of those tight quarters and preached to us every single day. But I'll tell you right now: your dad brought life to our platoon. It wasn't just what he said. It was what he did. He lived each word he preached. Every single man of us knew Jesus was real, that He was the Son of God, and that He had died for our 'wretched' souls. Wretched was the word he used. And by the time your dad got through describing us, as he knew us, because of how close our quarters were, we knew we needed Jesus."

"Sounds like my dad, every day of the week. I can't get by with anything. Sometimes, I think he knows what I am going to do before I have any idea I might do it." Clay ran his finger around the rim of his coffee cup.

"You know, Boy, your dad walks with a limp. That limp is because of me."

Clay looked at the man, but the man was gazing back into the distance of time. "I got shot through the side and left on the battlefield. I can still smell the smoke, and even now, that smoke burns my eyes. As I lay there, not knowing if I was going to live or die, the man who shot me was coming on a run. I tried to grab my rifle, but I threw it wide when I fell. Just as I rolled over to reach and catch it in my grip, that soldier jumped and stood astride of me. His eyes held fire and fear. I don't think I will ever forget them. He shoved his rifle right over my heart and fired. I thought I was dead, but I didn't see Heaven. His Mauser had jammed. I still think my heart stopped. I grabbed his leg and yanked, but I had lost all my strength on that side. I could not pull him down, but it threw him off balance. He twisted his Mauser around and raised it to chunk me in the head, and I knew then heaven was coming. That's when your dad yelled that cowboy yee-hawing cry of his and sprang from behind. Oh, they rolled and fought. Thank the Lord, your dad won. He threw me up over his shoulder, and he tore out for our foxhole. He dropped me in, and just as he was following suit, he took a shot in the hip." Mr. Kent smiled. "From then on, your dad walked the straight and narrow with a crooked stride."

They both laughed.

Looking back in time, Mr. Kent paused. "That battle sent both of us home. At least we made it home," he whispered. "Some of ours didn't make it. But…most of our platoon called Jesus their Lord and Saviour. And that was because of your dad. He's quite a man. I think the world of him and thank the Lord for him."

Clay hadn't heard that story before, and it made his heart yearn for his dad.

Mr. Kent dropped his hands to his knees. "Boy, I am bushed. Would you mind if I crashed at your cabin?"

Clay nodded, "Sure. I'll show you the way." He stood and looked toward the swinging kitchen door. Beep had stepped out. He turned to Mr. Kent, "Wait for me outside, and I'll be along in a minute."

Mr. Kent followed his eyes and winked. "Take as long as you like, Boy. I'll find a bench."

Clay stood, pushed his chair beneath the table, and walked over to Beep. "You got a minute to talk?"

Beep looked about the dining room and nodded. "Meet me out the back door."

Clay tipped his hat, turned, and left. He stopped to nod at Mr. Kent and to tell Ole Honker to stay. "I'll be back shortly."

Ole Honker whined, but he obeyed. The dog lay down and sniffed Mr. Kent. Then he lay his head on his paws.

Clay pulled a biscuit from his pocket and gave it to his dog, his friend. "Good Boy, Ole Honker. You stay and keep Mr. Kent company. He's a good man. You can trust him."

Ole Honker swallowed the biscuit whole and whined for more.

Clay laughed. "When I get back, Boy, when I get back. You be good for Mr. Kent."

Clay looked up and down the street before he stepped off the boardwalk and into the alley. Alleys were spooky. That is where mean dogs hid, drunks slept it off, and rats roamed. It was also where he had chased the man from last night. There were a bunch of banged-up garbage cans, but no one was hiding between them. It was daylight, and now he could see. Clay went through the alley and to the back door. The door hung open, letting cool air in through the screen door. He knocked softly.

Beep looked behind her before she slipped out.

"Did you tell your granny about your papa?" he asked.

She shook her head. "Not yet."

"Beep, she's got to know."

"I know that, but there wasn't time this morning, and she insisted on getting over here to cook. She loves this job and her customers. Well, most of them, anyway. They love her, too, as well as her food. I think even your 'Puty Sneedle likes her." She giggled at the name. "Deputy Sneedle is a regular every morning as soon as the door is opened, and the welcome mat is laid."

"That's why you didn't come to open the door and lay out the mat today? Deputy Sneedle? Were you scared?"

Fire shot from her eyes. "Yes, I was, and I am scared. But, believe me, he had better be more scared of me. I am going to get proof and tell the whole world what he did."

"Beep, you've got to be careful. You know what he did to your papa, and I don't know what he'll do to you if he gets a chance. I think he's crazy," Clay warned.

"If he is crazy, all of Rocky Branch needs to know it. He is their deputy. They need to know that he thinks he can make the law into anything he wants it to be."

Clay shook his head. "I agree with you, but you have got to be careful. He is dangerous and even more so if he is crazy. We need to pray before we act."

"To God? Do you really think I want to pray to God? Look what He let happen to my papa?" Tears seemed to jump from her eyes and cascade down her face. She took her apron and slashed them away.

Clay felt his heart drop. "Beep, you don't mean that. You can't mean that."

"Really? Clay, that was my papa. You saw what happened to him. I needed him. My granny needed him. How do you think I should feel?" Beep trembled.

"Beep, I don't know, but not mad at God," he whispered. "The God I know loves you."

She pressed her lips together, "Then we must not know the same God." She whirled to go back inside.

Clay caught her arm. "Wait, Beep."

She looked up at him with vacant eyes. "Why?'

"Because I want to help."

She looked him up and down. "If you come to help, are you bringing your God?"

"Beep, I never go anywhere without him. He lives in me." Clay spoke softly.

"Was he with you last night when 'Puty Sneedle murdered my papa?"

Clay nodded, "Yes. He never leaves me."

She wildly dragged in a breath, "Then if he is God, why didn't he stop 'Puty Sneedle from shooting my papa?"

"Beep, I don't know the answer to that question, but I know God did not let 'Puty Sneedle shoot you, me, or Ole Honker. And God let us get out on the river before 'Puty Sneedle could shoot us or drill holes in my boat. And God took care of your granny. And I know God has sent us help."

She glared, "If your God let you lose someone you love, you wouldn't think your God was so high and mighty."

Clay narrowed his eyes, "Really? Do you really think that, Beep? My mom has been gone for five years. She took a fever, and the fever took her. I can't even put flowers on her grave because my dad and I left her way back in Kansas, deep in the sod under the sunset sky. I can't talk to her, but do you know what I can do?" The boy didn't wait for an answer from the girl. "I ask my God to hug my mom and tell her that I love her and miss her. I'll bet the sunset she is looking down on is much more brilliant than the one I am looking up at. And I haven't seen my dad in over a week now…" He choked on the tears he refused to cry because boys don't cry. He looked above her head and far into nowhere.

Beep slipped her hand in his and sobbed, "I am so sorry, Clay. I'm just not so sure about your God."

Clay nodded.

"Will you forgive me?" she whispered.

Again, he nodded. Still, it was too hard to talk.

Granny opened the screen door. She held a wooden spoon in her hand and shook it as she preached. "I know your talk has something to do with God because I have heard his name a few times. Both of you had best be respecting his name."

Clay swallowed, "Yes, Ma'am."

Beep looked to the ground.

"Mmm," Granny stood with her hands on her hips. "Bee Poppy says if'n I let her off this afternoon, it would give her some time. She has a plan to go back out on the river where she lost sight of her papa last night. Only this time, it will be daylight. I told her no, but she said you might go with her. Is that right? Would you go with my Bee Poppy?" Granny's eyes could dig right into the heart of your soul.

"I'd be honored to take Beep out on the river," Clay told her.

"Beep?" Granny raised her eyebrows in question.

Clay shrugged. "I call her Beep. It's a whole lot easier to say."

Granny chuckled, "Well, now, Bee Poppy is a mouth load, and the girl will be heard. She never learned to keep her mouth shut, even for her own good."

Beep gasped, "Granny?"

Granny waved the spoon she was holding, "You know it's so. I'll let the two of you go, but no funny stuff. I won't have it." She shook her wooden spoon. "My man hasn't come home yet, and I want to know the why of it." Granny aimed the spoon at Clay, "If you'll take Beep with you and go, I'll be thanking you." She paused before she added, looking directly at Beep and pointing her wooden spoon, "I'll be a praying the Good Lord will go with you and lead the way." Granny winked and stepped back through the screen door, letting it slam to emphasize her feelings about her good Lord.

GONE!!!

Chapter #7

It was agreed. Beep's Granny would pack lunch while Clay took Mr. Kent to his cabin. The walk wasn't long, and Mr. Kent was quiet. Clay let him be quiet. Maybe he was tired, and maybe he was thinking. Clay glanced at him from beneath his hat. No. He recognized that look. His dad had carried that look many times. Mr. Kent was planning, and Clay did not think he would share that plan. If he were like Dad, he sure didn't want to interrupt his thoughts.

"The cabin's right between these trees," Clay ducked under damp tendrils of Spanish Moss to push aside branches. Clay had asked his dad about clearing the path to the cabin, but his dad had told him no. He liked being off the road, and he especially appreciated the seclusion it offered.

At the edge of the clearing, Ole Honker growled from deep within. The hair stood on his neck, and he pointed his nose toward the cabin.

The door hung open.

"Someone's…" Clay didn't finish. He ran to the cabin.

Mr. Kent shot out in front of the boy. He jumped the steps in one stride and hurled across the porch.

A Shot in the Night

A shot shattered the hush of the surrounding forest and whizzed by Mr. Kent's head. He dropped onto the porch slats and yelled. "Hit the ground, Boy. Now!"

Clay didn't have to be told twice. He dropped.

From within the cabin, three more shots roared out the door, and glass shattered. Someone dove out the side window, scrambled to their feet, and tore through the trees.

For as big as he was, Mr. Kent yanked himself off the porch floor and flew after the man, leaving his bowler hat spinning on its top.

Clay rolled over and sat up. Someone had been in his cabin, and maybe someone still was. "Dear Lord," he whispered, "what if I had come home alone?"

Clay's heart was pounding. Should he get up and go check out the cabin to see if someone else was still inside? He rubbed his hands up and down his thighs.

The wild crashing through the trees stopped, and Mr. Kent stepped out of the forest. He shoved his fingers through his hair with one hand and looked at Clay. "Gone. I lost him in those trees." His breath was rapid as he pointed behind. "Did you see anything, Clay?"

Clay stood on shaky legs and dusted the grass from his chest. "I didn't see his face, but I saw the back of him running like the coward he is. I'd know him front or back. It was 'Puty Sneedle."

"Sneedle? You sure?"

"I'm sure. Cross my heart," he crossed his heart with his finger, "and hope to die," he slid the side of his hand across his throat.

Mr. Kent grinned. "I figured it to have been Sneedle." He paused, catching his breath before he spoke again. "You know your dad did that heart/ throat thing, too."

"Still does. He taught me," Clay spat on the ground.

Mr. Kent studied the boy without a word.

But Clay knew what he was thinking. A heavy cloud slipped over him like a wet gunny sack thrown over his head. He looked Mr. Kent in the eye, "You're thinking my dad isn't coming back."

Mr. Kent did not drop his eyes. "I am saying a prayer for your dad and my friend, D'Gregory. The good Lord can pull him through anything."

Clay's eyes were filling up fast. He turned his head to the cabin so Mr. Kent couldn't see, but he figured Mr. Kent knew anyway.

The man didn't look at the boy. The boy needed a moment to collect those tears, and he would give him that. Mr. Kent focused on the gaping door. "How about we go check out the cabin and see what damage was done?"

Clay nodded and headed toward the steps. He stopped at the door to pull in a rugged breath. Three legs were broken from the toppled table, and the two cots were upside-down, with the blankets thrown in a pile. The pillows had been ripped apart, and their feathers had flown the coop…again. He swallowed, hoping to clear the tears because his heart was yanked in two when he settled his eyes on the quilt his mom had made. It was heaped in the far corner of the room, wearing what was left of the pot of beans that had been tossed in the middle of brightly colored patches. Canned goods kept on the shelf above the cooking stove littered the wooden boards.

Clay felt like sitting in the middle of the floor and bawling, but he was a man, and men did not cry.

Ole Honker sat and howled. Then the dog sniffed, catching the scent. He growled and followed it to the broken window. Whining, he placed his paws on the ledge and barked.

"No, Ole Honker. We can't follow him now. Not now," Clay ordered.

Ole Honker whined again, but he dropped from the windowsill and moseyed over to rest at his master's feet.

"Well, what do you make of this?" Mr. Kent asked as he stood looking down, rubbing his stubbly chin.

In the corner of the room stood Dad's bedside table with his Bible on top. Only the Bible was opened. Dad never left it open because he wanted the pages protected. His Bible had a knife stabbed clear through the pages, pinning a note on top of the

Word. Clay stepped over and read the note. "I no you wuz the kid frum last nite. I WANT THAT GIRL!"

Clay looked at Mr. Kent, "I've got to get to Beep."

Mr. Kent nodded, "I think that is a good idea. I'll tag along."

"No need. Beep's Granny has an errand she wants us to take care of. Kind of girl stuff. You would be bored." Clay tiptoed around the truth. If Mr. Kent really knew the errand they were making, he would not let them leave without him.

Mr. Kent nodded. "I would like a chance to go through this mess and look for clues. Everything is fresh right now. Are you sure you two will be fine on your own?"

"Sure thing." Clay absently ran his hand over the gun poked in the back of his waistband. He dropped his eyes to the floor. He didn't want Mr. Kent to ask him what the errand was for fear he would insist on going with them. Beep wouldn't like that, and he figured Mr. Kent might even make them stay in Rocky Branch while he went to check out the place on the river from last night.

Mr. Kent was still standing beside the stabbed Bible. He chuckled. "Wonder if 'Puty Sneedle realizes he stabbed God's Word, God's 'SWORD' with a mere knife? 'And take the helmet of salvation, and the sword of the Spirit, which is the word of God:' Ole Sneedle shot a fiery dart, but we have got the sword of God! That should put the fear of God into that Sneedle, if he had sense enough to fear God."

Clay tipped his head. "That's right." Courage built inside him. His dad had taught him all his life that the Word was his sword.

"Clay, when you get to that girl, do not leave her alone, not even for a minute. If she must visit the privy, you go with her and stand outside. That is the only time you are to let her out of your sight. Understand?"

"Yes, Sir," Clay swallowed. If Arthur Kent knew their plans, he would squelch them.

Mr. Kent turned back to the mess in the cabin. "I'll clean up this rubble, and I'll poke around some more for clues. After that, I'll come and check on the two of you, but whatever you do, don't leave Beep alone."

"I won't, I promise. Cross my heart," he crossed his heart, "and hope to die," he slid the side of his hand across his throat. The boy stepped to the door and stopped. Slowly, he turned back to Mr. Kent. He whipped away a stupid tear that showed itself and mumbled, "I would like to take my dad's sword."

Mr. Kent nodded. Tenderly, he pulled the knife from the pages, closed the book, and took it to the boy. "Might just be the best weapon you ever wield."

*****

A Shot in the Night

Beep was drying dishes, and her granny was sweeping the floor when Clay tapped on the screen door.

Granny looked up and smiled a welcome. "Come on in, but be sure your boots are clean. I just finished sweeping and mopping this kitchen, and the floor ought to be spic and span."

"Yes, Ma'am," Clay felt the need to take his hat off in her presence.

Ole Honker wagged his tail in time to his yelping. He wanted to go in.

"Stay, Ole Honker. I'm sure Granny doesn't want the likes of you in her kitchen," Clay warned.

"I surely don't. Dogs track in who knows what all, and dogs stick their wet nose on everything in sight, and that ain't clean," Granny stepped through the door and hung her mop against the outside wall on a peg. She glared at the dog, but she pulled something wrapped in a dishcloth from her apron pocket. "Dogs," Granny's brows were furrowed, but she unwrapped a bone and shoved it toward Ole Honker, then yanked it back. "Now, you listen to me. I don't want any bone slivers left on my step or anything that could get tracked onto my clean kitchen floor. Do you hear me, Dog?"

Ole Honker sat up and yelped.

"Good. We understand each other." She sniffed, handed over the bone, and stepped back inside.

Clay's eyes were big, but he didn't say a word. He looked at Beep.

Beep whispered, "Granny's all bark and no bite."

Both snickered.

"I heard that, and I do bite." Granny glared.

Clay choked on his laughter.

Beep held her tummy.

Granny eyed them both and finally joined the fun with a chuckle.

When they had settled down, Granny said, "I want both of you front and center."

Clay watched Beep cross to stand in front of her granny. He did the same.

Granny propped one hand on her hip and pointed the other at both Beep and Clay. "I want you to always stay together, and I want you back before dark. Understand?"

"Yes, Ma'am," Beep said.

Clay nodded, "Yes, Ma'am."

Granny looked toward the ceiling. She held her hand to her chest, her eyes misty, "Mostly, I want you to come back with your papa. We been married coming on 47 years, and I don't want to celebrate without him."

Celebrate? Clay was afraid to breathe, and he was afraid to look at Beep for fear of spilling their secret.

How were they going to tell Granny that her husband was dead? Was Beep planning to bring back her papa's body and say, "Granny, this is what we found?" He swallowed the lump in his throat that must be his heart.

Beep answered, "Yes, Ma'am."

Finally, Clay slid his eyes Beep's way. Her fists were knotted, and she was trembling.

Granny didn't seem to notice. She handed them a small hamper. "Your lunch is packed in this, and I put some ointment and rags in if you should need them for your papa." She shook her head. "That man is always getting nicked on something or finding poison oak."

"Yes, Ma'am," Clay said and took the hamper. He sure had said 'yes, Ma'am' a whole bunch of times since he had met Granny.

Granny held up her finger in the air as if she had just remembered something. "Wait here." She went to the pantry and came out toting a quilt. "Beep, if your papa went to work today with no rest last night, he is going to be plumb tuckered out. That is when the fever hits a body. He'll sure be a shivering something awful. Wrap him up tight in this quilt, even if he doesn't want you to. It will keep him warm until I can get some hot soup down him." She handed the quilt to Beep.

Beep splashed a tear on the quilt.

Granny scooped her up in a warm hug. "Sweetie, your papa be in God's mighty hands, and there is no better place to be. Our God will take care of him."

Clay didn't know if Beep had heard or not. She was shaking, and the tears were rolling.

Granny looked over Beep's head. "Young Man, I want you to take care of my little lady here and her papa when you find him. I know you are a good man."

Clay did not feel like a good man. He was only 13, and he knew sometimes you had to be a man before your time because his dad had been telling him that since his mom had passed. But he didn't feel like a man, much less a good man. He felt like a liar. Dad had drilled it into him that a man does not lie. Guilt felt like it had spread all over his face. He dropped his gaze from Beep's granny.

Granny reached over, and with her finger under his chin, she raised his head to look him eye-to-eye. "I want your promise, Young Man."

She left no room for anything but agreement.

Clay felt like saluting her, but instead, he nodded and whispered, "Yes, Ma'am."

Immediately, Granny dropped her head. "Dear Lord God, Almighty, we as your servants come before your throne to beg you to send your whole staff of angels before, behind, and beside these children. Keep them safe and help them find my man, George. I know he is your man, and you have shared him with me these many years, but I'm not ready to give him up yet. I beg you, Jesus, keep them all safe, my Beep, this Young Man, Clay, and even that ole dog, Ole Honker."

Clay slid a peek at Granny.

Granny winked.

Clay dropped his mouth wide, then dropped his head.

Granny continued, "Please, bring them back to me. It is in your Holy name I be asking, amen."

Beep was sobbing.

Tenderly, Granny took the hem of her apron and dabbed Beep's cheeks. Clay heard her whisper, "God knows right where your papa be. He'll lead you to him, and he'll bring you safe back again. It's all in his big, strong hands. You just got to trust Him to it."

"But, Granny, what…what if…if God doesn't have it?" the girl choked between sobs.

"Honey, God always has it. It's us'ns what don't always have it. That's why God tells us to grow in faith. He can see what's ahead of us. We can't, but he holds our hand to carry us through. 'Member the Children of Israel moaning and groaning at the Red Sea with the whole Egyptian army storming up behind them? They couldn't stand still, and they couldn't keep their mouths shut until those mighty waters rolled apart." Granny chuckled. "I bet they quieted down then. I wished I could have seen it. I bet Moses didn't have to tell them twice to get a move on and step into that sea. The Promised Land was closer than ever." She shook her head, "But that ole Pharaoh and his army of unbelievers, they never saw the Promised Land. They had plague after plague, chance after chance to believe, and they didn't. And finally, God let them march right into the midst of the Red Sea, and then God withdrew his hands. Our Lord God Almighty let the waters of the Red Sea swallow them all!"

Clay felt like he was listening to one of Dad's sermons, and he didn't dare to interrupt.

Granny stepped back and took a deep breath. "Well, we're burning daylight, and I want you back before dark." Then, very seriously, she added, "Even if you can't find Papa, I want you back before dark."

Chills traveled up Clay's back as he rested his eyes on Granny's. She already knew Beep's papa, and her man was gone!

The Black Hole

Chapter #8

Clay slapped at a mosquito trying to grab lunch, and Ole Honker wiggled his ears to shoo the bloodthirsty pests away. Beep was cuddled in Granny's quilt. Maybe she did it to keep the mosquitoes at bay, but it made Clay sweat. There was no way Beep could be cold, but she was broken-hearted, and that might make a girl want to cuddle. Clay pulled his gaze away from Beep to watch the river. They had to be getting close to where 'Puty Sneedle had shot Beep's Papa. Clay slowed his rowing. A turtle family slid off a log close to the boat and dove for the deep, popping their heads up further away from the newcomers. Birds gossiped back and forth across the river, warning all river critters of the intrusion.

Behind the turtle log, there was a giant splash from the bank. Ole Honker popped his head up and growled. An alligator slithered into the water and across the river. Ole Honker kept guard, his tail sashaying in rhythm with the alligator's tail. As the reptile reached the other side, Ole Honker barked a victory call.

"Whoa, Boy. Don't rock the boat," Clay warned. "No one wants to be alligator lunch today, and if you see one alligator, you can know there are a dozen."

Ole Honker whined, but he sat back down.

Clay sighed, "Beep, we need to talk."

"I know," she whispered.

"Why didn't you tell your granny what happened last night?"

"Why? How? What was I supposed to do? Was I going to tell her that 'Puty Sneedle shot Papa, and then that horrible murderer tried to snatch a hold of me? Granny would have panicked. She would have wanted to grab the lanterns, find any kind of boat she could get to, and go in search of Papa." She spread her hands wide, dropping the quilt from her shoulders. "When we found Granny, she was on the floor of the cabin, and I didn't know what kind of shape she was in. I had just lost Papa. I thought I was going to lose Granny, too. I even thought that if I told her, she might keel over and die." She looked up at Clay with wild eyes, "What would you have done?"

He shrugged, "I don't know, maybe the same thing you did. But how are you going to tell her you already knew he was…" Clay paused. He didn't know how to say her Papa was dead. Finally, he winced and blurted it out, "How are you going to tell her you knew all along he was dead, and you didn't tell her?"

It was her turn to shrug. "Maybe I won't have to."

"Sometime, Beep, you are going to have to tell her." He dragged his oar through the deep water. "I think we are getting close," Clay spoke quietly.

Beep looked and shivered, "It's right around this bend. Papa knew where he was going. He didn't tell me that, but I watched him follow marks in the trees. I think he knew who had put the marks there, or he suspected."

"You think he suspected 'Puty Sneedle?"

"If Papa didn't suspect him, I do," she swallowed.

"You know we need to be on the lookout for 'Puty Sneedle."

"In the daylight?" Beep shook her head. "I've watched him around Rocky Branch. He's the lawman, and he likes the attention it gives him. He stands a little taller, especially when the ladies nod at him and call him Deputy Sneedle."

Clay nodded, "I noticed that, too." He had seen him soaking up the way people treated their lawmen. They always gave him a smile and praise. "You are right about that. So, you are saying he saves the river work for the night?"

"Yep. Besides, 'Men love darkness rather than light because their deeds are evil.'"

"So, you do know the scriptures."

Beep glared at the boy. "You listened to my granny."

Clay laughed and dipped his oar into the deep waters. "Why did your Papa bring you with him last night?"

Beep dropped her eyes. "Honestly, he didn't. I wanted to come, but he said no. So, I went to bed early, crawled out my window, and waited to see which direction he would take. Then I followed. We were far enough away from Rocky Branch when Papa spotted me. He gave me 'what for,' but he didn't want me going home alone in the deep of night, and he was determined to find what he was looking for." She shrugged, "He had to let me tag along."

"What was he looking for?" Clay asked.

Beep shook her head, "He never said. When we almost ran into 'Puty Sneedle, Papa whipped around, smothered his hand over my face, and mouthed the word, "QUIET!" That's how I know 'Puty Sneedle was who Papa was trying to find. We hid, and then we followed him."

Clay looked at Beep. The color had drained from her face, and silence took over the conversation. The boat glided through the water, and birds chattered. Every now and again, a bullfrog dove into the river, making a splash.

Tears salted Beep's cheeks again, and Clay wondered how many tears a girl could cry. He remembered his mom saying that God keeps your tears in a bottle. Clay smiled. "Beep, God must have a big bottle with your name on it."

She dragged her hands across her face, sliding the tears away, and looked up at Clay, "Why?"

"My mom taught me that I should never be ashamed of crying because there is a verse in Psalms that says, 'Thou tellest my wanderings: put thou my tears into thy bottle: are they not in thy book?'"

"God says that?" Beep sounded doubtful.

"He sure does, in Psalms 56:8."

"You cry?"

Clay gazed into the distance. "I try not to. I am getting better, but my mom said sometimes men cry." He didn't look at the girl, but he had to swallow some sort of sob before he continued. "My dad cried when my mom died, and they said, 'ashes to ashes and dust to dust,' and then he took the shovel to throw dirt on the casket to tuck her into the ground."

Both Beep and Clay fought to dam back the tears as the boat glided over the water.

Ole Honker whined.

Clay steadied his oar to stop the boat. He whispered, "Beep, I think this is the place. It looks different in the daylight, but I'm sure this is it."

Beep studied the bank and nodded, "Just behind that big black gum tree is where I think 'Puty Sneedle crouched to shoot Papa."

Clay stirred the waters, turning the boat toward the bank. They glided to the edge of the water. Clay hopped out and tethered the boat. He stretched out his hand to help Beep as she jumped. Ole Honker whined and soared through the air, following them.

Beep was shaking.

Ole Honker was sniffing a trail that led to the black gum tree.

The black gum tree looked eerie, with moss hanging from its branches and brushing the ground.

Clay swiped his hands down his sides and turned to Beep. "Guess this is where the trail leads." He held the stringy moss aside for Beep to duck under.

"You want me to go first?" she asked.

Clay grinned, "Girls first."

Beep glared. "I am not afraid," she said, but she was. Beep ducked under, and then he followed. It was damp and dark, and when the moss dropped, they were separated from the world.

Clay followed Ole Honker, and together, they walked slowly about the circumference of the tree, Ole Honker sniffing and Clay stepping carefully so as not to destroy the sign. Just inside the hanging moss, he found where someone had knelt, but he followed Ole Honker to the tree trunk, where he noticed tracks all around the base of the black gum tree. A chunk of moss had been knocked loose from the big, low-hanging branch where it connected to the trunk. Clay stepped over and stood on his tiptoes. Shivers went up his spine. There was a hole in the tree, but in this part of the forest, almost any kind of animal could be in that hole home. He did not want to tangle with any of them.

Ole Honker lay down panting in the cool debris from years of the tree shedding.

Clay stared at the dark hole.

"What did you find?" Beep asked.

"Some kind of hole home or maybe a stash hole."

"What is in it?" she asked.

Clay looked at the girl, "You crazy? There is no way I am going to poke my hand in that dark hole."

"You scared?" she asked.

"Give me a good reason I shouldn't be scared. Snakes and spiders and bats and who knows what all else live in hole homes in trees," he challenged.

Beep stepped up to the tree trunk. She was short and couldn't even get high enough to look around the side of the branch to see the dark hole. "Give me a leg up," she said.

"No. I will not be responsible for your death," he told her.

She rolled her eyes, and only the whites of her eyes flashed in the deep shadows of the black gum tree. "And how will I die?"

"If there is a moccasin snake in that hole and you get bitten, you'll die. Your hand will turn purple and swell up, and then your arm, and then the rest of you. Your lungs will explode, and that is all she wrote!"

Beep shivered. "Maybe you could poke a stick in the hole?"

Clay narrowed his eyes, "Me?"

She shrugged and smiled, "You probably move faster than me." She kicked around in the layers of decay beneath the tree, looking for a good stick. Something shiny caught in the shaft of light between two branches. She knelt. "Look, Clay." She picked up the brass casing from a rifle shot and held it for him to examine.

Clay whistled, "Well, if that don't beat all."

"You think that is evidence?"

"If we could prove it came from the same rifle that shot your Papa, it would be evidence. I don't know if they can do that or not, but we are going to keep it." He shoved the brass into his pocket. "Let's go find your Papa."

"What about the dark hole?" Beep asked and handed him a stick from the ground.

He grimaced, but he took the stick. He was not a coward, and he would prove it. With a deep breath, he poked it in the hole. "There's something in there," he whispered and poked a bit harder.

With a wild screech, an irate squirrel tore out of the black hole, flying toward Clay.

A scream like a girl blasted from the boy as Clay vaulted backward, batting at the frenzied beast with the stick. The boy landed on his behind with the squirrel on top of his chest, running for his face. Clay grabbed the wad of deadly fur and threw it as far as he could.

The squirrel torpedoed through the air into Beep's hair and caught hold. Beep danced in circles, screaming like a banshee. The squirrel lost its grip and was flung into the tree trunk, where Ole Honker lunged for the animal. The dog bit down on the squirrel's tail, and the squirrel clamped onto Ole Honker's ear, the same ear that had been shot last night. Ole Honker yowled, letting go of his prey. The squirrel released Ole Honker's ear and dove for the tree trunk, which the squirrel gladly scrambled up into the highest branches of the black gum tree, then sat and scolded those below.

Beep whirled about and pointed at Clay, yelling, "You threw that monster beast on me!"

Clay was rolling with laughter.

Ole Honker stood with his front paws up on the tree trunk, whining.

The squirrel was ranting and railing from the top branches of the black gum tree, its tail standing up and over at a 90-degree bend in the middle of its tail where Ole Honker had latched on.

Beep stood with her hands on her hips and stomped. "Well, now that the beast is gone, I guess you won't be afraid to dig in the dark hole."

Clay sat up. He did not want to dig in the dark hole, but he did not want her to call him a coward either. He stood and slapped the damp debris from his trousers. With a deep breath, he stuck his hand into the hole.

From behind, Beep grabbed him and yelled.

Clay's heart jumped into his throat, and he was glad. If his heart had not blocked his throat, he would have bellowed so loud that all of Louisiana would have heard him and come running. He whipped about and pointed a shaking finger at the girl, but she had turned white. "What?" he asked.

She pointed at his feet. A piece of paper floated past and landed on top of a worn work glove. "That is Papa's glove. See, the little finger is torn off. Papa caught it in a saw blade, and we were so thankful it only yanked off the little finger from the glove." Tenderly, Beep picked up the glove.

Clay nabbed the paper and unfolded it. His heart tapped a little faster. "Beep, listen to this: 'Take care of this man. Come back tomorrow, and there will be more.'"

Beep held the glove to her chest, then yanked it away. She reached her hand into the glove and pulled out a treasure. She spread her fingers wide, and in her palm lay five twenty-dollar gold pieces.

Clay looked Beep in the eye. "'Puty Sneedle was paid to kill your papa." Nervously, he looked around. "'This means "Puty Sneedle will be back today."

Beep nodded.

Clay watched her cry. Tears. That bottle God kept for her was getting fuller all the time.

He's Gone!

Chapter # 9

Clay grabbed Beep's arm. "I know 'Puty Sneedle loves all the attention he gets on his day job, Beep, but this is a lot of money. We need to face the facts. "Puty Sneedle might be headed for this very tree right now. We need to clear out of here, and the faster the better."

Beep nodded but pulled away from Clay. "Let's get shut of this tree, yes. But I can't go without getting my papa. Granny has to have him."

Clay swallowed. Shivers were traveling over his body. Last night had been unbelievable, but it was also unplanned. Today, they knew what might happen, and it seemed like they were making a beeline right into the danger zone. "Beep, your papa's body has got to be close to here. We need to get him and get clean out of this hunk of river land."

Beep took a step away from the boy. "You don't have to come if you are scared, but I will not leave my papa another day lying out on the ground for some critter to come and eat away. Last night, I didn't have a choice, but today is another story. Today, I have a choice. I don't want to leave him lying another day and have that haunting my conscience until the day I die."

"Scared?" Clay's voice squeaked on the word. "Sometimes being scared will save your life. And now," he looked deep into her eyes, "we are not talking about squirrels. We are talking about 'Puty Sneedle, who carries a rifle, a handgun, and a knife that I know of. Plus, he has a badge to hide behind. It would be pure crazy to stay here."

Beep backed away. "Then call me pure crazy because we are this close," she threw her hand in the air and measured about one-half of an inch with her fingers, "to where 'Puty Sneedle shot my papa. And I will not leave until I find his body."

"OH!" Clay yanked his hat off and whopped his leg with it. "Girls!" He tromped to the hanging moss of the tree and threw a chunk of it to the side. He waited for the girl to duck under the hole in the moss he held. "After you, Miss," he growled.

Ole Honker whined and followed Beep.

"Trader," Clay hissed at his dog who whined and followed Beep. The boy dropped the moss he held, sighed and stepped after them.

With his long strides, Clay caught up with his dog and Beep. Silence ruled the air as neither wanted to talk with the other, and Ole Honker had nothing to say except with the flip of a tail.

Ole Honker stopped, pointed, and whined.

Beep saw the spot. She ran but came to a standstill. She gasped. Slowly, she turned in a circle. "He's gone!" she gasped.

Clay stepped into the clearing beneath the bent pine. He looked about. This was the place, he was sure. He began casting for sign. He pointed to a mound of leaves, and with the toe of his boot, he pushed them aside. "Beep, see this?" he asked.

"Yes," she whispered.

"This is where your papa fell, and this," he pointed with the stick he still held from the fight with the psycho squirrel, "And this is blood." A dark spot stained the damp dirt.

Beep gasped, "Maybe Papa wasn't dead? Maybe he was just unconscious? He might be wandering in these woods, hurt, and all alone."

Clay slid his hat from his head as his soft eyes fell on the girl. "Beep," he spoke gently, rolling the brim of his hat, "your papa was shot between the eyes. I saw him, and believe me, no one lives through that."

"Are you sure?"

"I'm sure, Beep. I'm sure."

And she was crying again.

"That jar in Heaven is getting bigger," the boy whispered.

Ole Honker whined.

Clay slipped over to the girl and put his arm about her shoulders. "It's ok to cry. It cleanses your soul from your sorrows. God planned it that way."

"But now, what am I going to do? What am I going to tell Granny? And now I really don't know what happened to him, so I can't tell her he died."

Beep wrapped her arms about herself and began to rock.

"You do know he was shot, and you know he died. That would be the best place to start with your granny," Clay told her. "Your granny deserves to know."

Beep flopped her hands at her sides. "I can't tell her."

"You can't not tell her. She'll keep looking for him to show up. Besides, I think she already knows," Clay sighed.

"What? She knows he is dead? How could she know?" Beep paused, thinking of possibilities. She whirled around to face Clay. "Unless you told her!"

"Beep, I didn't tell her. I looked into her eyes, and I thought she knew. I could bet money she knew. I think it's like when God's Word says, 'The two shall become one.' She knows half of her is gone."

The girl dropped her head.

"Beep, look, let's follow the sign. We might be able to figure out what happened to him." Clay told her.

Slowly, Clay squatted and neither talked. With his eyes, he followed a faint trail toward the river. He stood. "Beep, look at this." He pointed toward the river. "It is like a road map of what happened."

She squinted, "A map? How? I don't see anything."

Clay pointed, "Look at the leaves. Most of them are well packed down from the weather. The rain soaks them. They rot and flatten out. They press against each other, but do you see where they seem to be fluffier?"

She nodded.

"I will bet we can find a trial underneath that fluff where your papa was dragged."

Beep followed the trail of fluff and gasped. "Into the river? He was drug into the river?"

Clay brushed the leaves aside and studied the ground beneath. "Beep, yes, it looks like he was drug to the edge of the water and shoved over the bank."

"'Puty Sneedle? You think he is the one who dragged Papa?"

Clay shrugged. He knew it could also have been an alligator, but he didn't know if that would make her feel any better. He didn't want her to think about what alligators would do with her papa's dead body.

But she did. Beep gasped, "Could it have been alligators?"

Clay could hear panic surging in her voice.

He shrugged. "I suppose it could, but chances are it was 'Puty Sneedle. He wouldn't want any evidence, and a body would definitely be evidence." He walked beside the path where the body had been dragged, studying the ground, and found what he was looking for. "Beep, see this?"

She nodded.

"That is a boot print." He pointed with his stick. "If we had 'Puty Sneedle's boot, we could match it. Besides, we were here, and you saw everything that happened before you ran away. That makes you an eyewitness."

Clay's heart began pounding. Not only was she an eyewitness, but now she was also the main target. 'Puty Sneedle would want her out of the way.

Horror filled Beep's eyes. She trembled. "That means he will kill me, doesn't it?"

Clay nodded, "I think he will try."

Ole Honker was nosing in the reeds and rushes at the river's edge. He whined, grabbed something, and wagged his tail. Proudly, he pranced to Beep and dropped the red and black hat he carried in his jaws at her feet.

Beep snatched it up and held it to her chest. "Papa's hat," she whispered.

"Who makes hats like that?" Clay frowned.

Beep looked at him with disgust, "It is a Tam O'Shanter hat from Scotland, and Papa has worn it as long as I have known him, maybe forever."

Clay nodded, "Scotland?" He shrugged, "Nice colors."

Ole Honker growled lowly in warning.

An airy whistle floated through the trees.

They froze.

Clay mouthed the words, "We have got to get out of here!"

Beep nodded and smashed her papa's hat tight on her head.

Clay took her hand, and they began winding through the trees away from the airy whistle and toward their boat.

They heard the man step into the crime scene and halt his airy whistle. "Someone's been here, and not long ago."

Clay yanked Beep's hand and hissed, "Run! We have got to get to the boat and out on the water!"

They crashed through the trees and brush, madly dashing across the distance.

The man followed. "I hear you! Now I see you! Stop! I'll shoot!"

A branch snatched Beep's hat from her head. Madly, she stopped, grabbing it.

"Leave it," Clay shouted.

"I will not, but she didn't take the time to smash it on her head again. She clutched it in one hand, and her papa's hat seemed to wildly follow her through the trees.

They dashed by the black gum tree, and the squirrel with the deformed tail scolded them.

Ole Honker stopped, growled, and yelped a warning to the squirrel.

"Not now, Ole Honker, come on!" Clay ordered.

The dog whined.

A shot fired, slapping through the trees. The squirrel dropped her treasured acorn, shrieked, and fled the scene. The acorn whapped Ole Honker on his snoot, and he sent a painful, moaning howl through the air.

The man with the gun stopped in his tracks. "What in tarnation was that? A wolf? A haunt?"

Clay ran faster.

Beep tore out after him, her hat tight in her hand but flinging of its own accord through the trees.

Then they heard the man gasp. "Tarnation! That old hat? That is the hat of George Washington Johnston, his own self. So…" He grabbed his heart. "That hat is dancing through the trees, through the air? That has to be the ghost of George Washington Johnston. Ain't nobody but Johnston has a hat like that. Tarnation! I'm chasing a haunt!" He spat on the ground beside his foot. "On my life, I will not chase a haunt. I am out of here!" He turned and blasted in the opposite direction through the forest.

Silence settled.

Clay and Beep were huffing as they jumped into the boat. Ole Honker howled before he dove in after them.

From a distance, they heard the man declare, "Ain't no job full of haunts worth no amount of money. The boss can do his own dirty work."

Clay wasted no time. He dipped the oars into the water and rowed. They had to get out of there, and the faster, the better.

Beep was holding her papa's hat on her head. She would not lose it. It had belonged to her papa, and it was a treasure, a piece of her papa she would keep close forever.

Ole Honker was panting. All his troubles were over. He lay his nose in Beep's lap and closed his eyes.

Clay broke the silence. "You were right. 'Puty Sneedle is not working alone. At least two others are working with him, the one who paid him to kill your papa and the one he paid to clean up his mess."

"But we don't know who either one is," Beep said.

Clay chuckled, "I didn't think it was a good idea to hang around and ask who he was."

Beep giggled, "I agree with you on that."

They sat in silence for a while.

Ole Honker snoozed and yapped in his sleep.

Beep laughed.

Clay smiled. "He does that, talks in his sleep. He probably was chasing the crooked-tailed squirrel from the black gum tree."

Again, Beep laughed. She asked, "Want a sandwich Granny sent?"

"You bet I do. With all that happened, I forgot about the hamper."

Beep opened the hamper, unwrapped the cloth from a sandwich, and handed it to Clay.

"Mmmm, homemade bread, butter, and strawberry jam. Your granny sure makes a good sandwich," Clay moaned with pleasure as he gulped down the last bite. "Got any more?"

Beep narrowed her eyes. "You ate that whole sandwich in three bites."

He licked his lips. "They were little slices of bread. Are there any more sandwiches?"

"One is for me, I'll have you know, Mr. Clay D'Gregory."

"I'll split it with you," he grinned.

She rolled her eyes, "Okay, there are two sandwiches left, but you are not getting my sandwich." She unwrapped the cloth and handed him another one.

Ole Honker whined.

"I hope you are happy, Clay. You just ate Ole Honker's sandwich," Beep scolded.

Clay laughed, "Your granny fixed a strawberry jam sandwich for a dog?"

"You don't think he'll eat it?" Beep asked.

"Oh, he would eat it, all right if he got a chance. He'll eat your shoes if he gets them when you aren't looking. Shoot, he'll eat the cloth the sandwiches were wrapped in if he gets a hold of it. He's a dog, and dogs will eat anything."

Beep grimaced, "Yuk." She turned away from Ole Honker to unwrap her sandwich.

Ole Honker nosed closer to the girl and begged. He drooled and whined.

"Alright," Beep pulled her sandwich in two and tossed half to the dog.

Honker gulped it down in one swallow.

Beep wrinkled her brow in amazement, "He didn't even chew."

Clay laughed.

Ole Honker moved closer to the girl, licked his jaws, and whined to beg for more.

"No, you old dog. This is mine," She jammed the sandwich in her mouth.

"And that is why I eat so fast," Clay chuckled.

When Beep had finished eating, she wiped her mouth with the cloth that had wrapped her sandwich. "Clay, we need help. I mean more help than just the three of us, but I am afraid to go to the sheriff. 'Puty Sneedle works for him."

Clay watched the sides of the river. He wanted to know if that man followed them from the shore. "Beep, do you remember the man I ate breakfast with?"

She nodded.

"I think we can trust him."

"Are you sure?"

"He knew my dad," Clay said as if that sealed the trust.

"Do you know how to find him?" Beep asked.

Clay licked his lips as he studied the distant waters, "I'm pretty sure he will find me."

The Tear Jar

Chapter #10

Evening shadows were draping the sky, and a couple of bright stars were sparking to catch a flame when Clay opened the gate for Beep into the yard of her cabin. The ground was swept clean, as most yards were, so that it wouldn't be an invitation to snakes and such unwanted varmints. Granny was waiting on the breezeway at the back kitchen door. One hand rested on her hip, and the other held a wooden spoon. Her lips were pressed together, and her eyebrows almost rose to her hairline. Her eyes beneath sparked with fire.

Clay had a tinge of fear. "Your granny always meet you this way?"

Beep shook her head, "It looks bad, but I figure she is worried more than anything."

Granny dropped her spoon and threw both hands over her heart. "You brought home Papa's hat, but not Papa?" Her shoulders sagged. "Just as I figured. I knew he was gone. The good Lord kept telling me not to expect him home."

Beep ran to her granny, and a few long minutes of hugging quietly melted into time. The sparking stars lit flames of fire against the soft black sky.

Clay didn't know if he should stay or go. It was a personal thing, and he was not a part of this family. It made him feel lonely. He kicked at the bare ground, feeling like it looked the way his heart probably looked, dry with nothing growing in it. He missed his mom and dad.

Ole Honker lay his head on Clay's feet and whined.

Clay thought his dog could feel it, too. He knelt and hugged his friend. "Ole Honker, Buddy. I thought I had lost you to that girl. I would've missed you, but I tell you what. I'd be glad to share you with her."

Ole Honker licked Clay's hand and whined.

"It's okay, Boy. Go get her," Clay scruffed his dog's neck.

Ole Honker made a beeline for Beep, his tail wagging, causing his back end to dance a boogie. The dog was not shy. He nosed between the two ladies and sat on both sets of feet.

Clay crossed his arms and smiled.

The two ladies laughed and stepped aside to let Ole Honker in between them.

Granny placed her hands on her hips and shook her head, "Trust an old hound dog to make light of things."

Beep knelt beside the dog and wrapped her arms about his neck. "Granny, his name is Ole Honker, and he's a good friend. He stuck with us today."

Clay stood in those evening shadows and looked away. Before long, he feared God might be opening the jar with his name on it to collect a few salty tears.

Granny looked at the boy standing in the gray light with his shoulders slumped. "So much sorrow on this earth," she whispered, shaking her head. "Heaven won't be that way. Young Man," she called, "Might as well come inside with us and give me a report."

Clay took a deep breath, threw his shoulders back, and answered, "Yes, Ma'am." The last thing he wanted to do was to give a report.

As soon as they were all inside, including Ole Honker, Granny shut the door and slid the deadbolt in place. "I don't intend to be disturbed tonight," she stated with a firm nod of the head. "We will sit around the table, and I have stew made, so we will eat while we talk."

Clay's stomach growled, even if he knew the talking might ruin the eating. "Sorry, Ma'am. I guess I'm hungry."

Beep poked him in the chest, "Why are you letting your tummy howl? You already had two sandwiches."

I'm a growing boy," he winked.

Granny laughed, "That is precisely why I fixed him two sandwiches, Bee Poppy. Now be a good girl and set the table."

Beep's mouth dropped open. "I set the table? What about him?" she pointed at Clay.

"He is going to wash his hands and face, and he is a guest," Granny pointed to the wash bowl. Then she narrowed her eyes, "Bee Poppy, you had best do the same. Both of you need it. I don't know where all you have been, and I don't want to know until we are sitting at the table."

Neither Beep nor Clay said a word. He followed her to the wash bowl and waited until Beep was done before he stuck his hands in the cool water. He stepped to the table when he had dried his hands and face with the towel.

Beep carried steaming bowls of stew and set them in place.

Granny balanced a pan of pone bread on her arm and nabbed a couple of glass jars filled with sweet tea. "Young Man, have a seat right here." She sat down the load of food she carried and waved her hand across the table. Then she turned to Beep. "I want you beside your friend. I want to look both of you in the eye while you report what you found." She pulled out her chair and sat.

Clay reached over and slid Beep's chair out for her, then turned and sat before Beep could tell him she could take care of her own chair.

Granny studied them both, took a hand of each, and bowed her head. "Dear Lord Almighty, we ask your blessing on this food, and whilst we partake of it, I ask that these two younguns will tell me the truth of what happened last night and today." She paused, cleared her throat, and started again with a slow, strong voice. "Help them to know that lies are of the Devil and only complicate the truth when Truth decides to reveal herself. Help them to remember lying is a sin against you."

Clay peeked across the table at Granny. Right now, he wasn't quite as hungry. Listening to her pray was almost like listening to his dad talk to the Lord. And Granny was tricky. She knew how to tangle words, so if you did lie, you were lying to God, not her. He slid a sneak peek at Beep.

Beep dropped her head in her hands, and Clay knew he was in trouble. He would follow Beep's lead, but she had better tell the truth.

"Amen," Granny said and smiled across the table at them. "Young man…"

Beep interrupted, "Granny, his name is Clay."

Granny nodded, "Clay, it is, then."

Ole Honker interrupted. He put his paws on Granny's lap and begged.

Granny dropped her gaze to the dog, and the boy was glad for the reprieve.

"Dogs do not eat at my table." Then she sighed, "Beep, go get him a bowl, break up some pone bread in it, and dip a bit of stew juice over it. Then, take it to the mat in front of the door for this poor beggar. I will not starve the hungry in my house, even if it be a dog."

Clay wanted to smile, but he did not want Granny to see him smile. He dropped his head to watch his bowl of steaming stew.

"Yes. Ma'am," Beep scooted from the table and did as she was bidden.

Gladly, Ole Honker followed her every step.

When Beep sat, Clay swiped a hunk of pone bread and tore it into chunks, dropping it into his stew. He took a bite and moaned, enjoying the savory morsel as it slid all the way to his tummy. He had been living on his and his dad's cooking for a long time now. Today, Beep's granny fed him breakfast, packed a hamper lunch, and now, supper. He whistled and chuckled, "God sure smiled on me today!"

Granny's eyes twinkled, "Just how did God do this smiling?"

Clay gulped. He had said that out loud without meaning to. Now, he had to explain it. "Ma'am, I was just thinking of your cooking. God blessed me with it three times in one day. It is the taste of heaven."

Beep glared at the boy and spoke through clenched teeth, "If you are trying to sweeten her up, you are barking up the wrong tree."

Clay sat up straight, "I mean it. You'd understand if you tried my cooking, and my dad's is not much better."

Granny was fast. "Where is your mother?"

The boy chewed and swallowed the food that now seemed to have grown into a lump. "She's with Jesus."

Granny reached across the table and patted his hand, which still clutched the spoon. "I am sorry, Son, and I am thankful you know she is with Jesus. I suspect His arms are the best place to be."

Clay swallowed the now tasteless bite. Sorrow sure could steal the joy of eating. He laid the spoon aside and knew Jesus had the lid open to the Jar with his name on it. He held his breath to keep from shedding those unwanted tears. Then he caught hold of Beep. She had stuck her spoon into her stew, settled her hands in her lap, and tears were pooling, ready to cascade over her cheeks.

Silence had settled like a thick fog. Granny looked to the ceiling, "Dear Father, please, be with us this night. All our hearts are drowning in sorrow, and you are the great Comforter. We need you." She shoved her bowl aside and crossed her arms on the table.

Ole Honker stopped licking his chops and growled. His hair on his back stiffened.

Hearts skipped a beat, and everyone at the table looked to the door.

There was a light tap.

No one breathed.

The knock sounded a bit louder.

Clay swallowed, "Ma'am, do you want me to get it?"

Granny did not answer; she clutched the neck of her blouse.

Clay was the man around here, so he stood and quietly eased to the door, "Who is it?"

Silence strung out for a few minutes, and Clay was glad Granny had bolted the door. Quickly, he looked across the room to see that the other door was bolted.

Again, the tapping sounded, but this time, it was followed by a whisper, "You don't know me, but my name is Arthur Kent. I would like to consider myself a friend."

Clay's sigh of relief swept over the room as he nodded at the ladies, "He's safe."

Granny took a deep breath, "Then, open the door, but bolt it the minute he is inside."

Arthur Kent stepped over the threshold and swept his hat from his head. "Thank you for trusting me."

Granny stood, "A friend of this Young Man is a friend of ours. Have you eaten?"

"No, Ma'am, and it smells mighty good." He gave that mouthy, white-toothed smile that seemed to melt hearts.

And it did. Granny beamed, "Mr. Kent, the wash bowl is right over there, and Beep will grab you a bowl of stew. I'll get a glass of tea."

Around the table, Mr. Kent brought security and comfort.

Granny smiled, "Ask, and ye shall receive."

Beep tipped her head to the side, "What?"

Granny's smile lit her eyes, "I asked the good Lord for comfort, and if I'm not mistaken, Mr. Kent carries the Comforter with him."

Arthur Kent put his hand over his heart. "Yes, Ma'am, I do. He lives in my heart."

"'The Spirit itself beareth witness with our spirit, that we are the children of God:' It says that in the book of Romans, chapter eight. I can tell that this man knows the Lord and is sent by our Lord." Granny turned to the man, "It is a pleasure to meet you, Mr. Kent."

"The pleasure is mine, Mrs. Johnston."

Granny's head popped up, "You know my name?"

"Yes, Mrs. Johnston, I know your name, and I am sorry." He spoke gently," I am afraid I come with bad news."

"About my husband?" Granny asked.

"Yes, Ma'am." His smile was kind.

"Do you know what has become of him?"

Mr. Kent laid his spoon down and clasped his hands together on the edge of the table. "We think he may have been in a fishing accident and did not fare well."

Beep jumped to her feet and leaned over the table. "He was not in a fishing accident. 'Puty Sneedle shot him in cold blood."

Arthur Kent leaned back in his chair. "How do you know this?"

"I know this because I was with my papa when 'Puty Sneedle shot him. Then 'Puty Sneedle tried to get a hold of me, and he was going to kill me, too."

Granny grasped her neck.

"He was going to kill you?" Mr. Kent questioned.

"Yes."

"Are you sure?" Mr. Kent leaned in.

"Mr., I saw him murder my papa. The only way he could shut me up would be to kill me. Now, if you want to know if he said he was going to kill me? Well, then the answer would be no. I didn't stick around to ask if that was what he meant when he tried to get a hold of me. I kicked him in the head as hard as I could, and I ran."

"You kicked him in the head? He's a tall man. How could you kick him in the head?" Mr. Kent asked.

"I'll tell you how. 'Puty Sneedle tripped over my papa's body and tumbled with him, so I kicked him in the head. I wish I had had a gun. I would have shot him in the head, right between the eyes, like he did to my papa. But I didn't have a gun, so I kicked him in the head instead, and then I ran. That's when I smacked into Clay."

Mr. Kent raised his eyebrows and studied Clay. "You were there when all this happened?"

"Yes, Sir."

"You were there, and you didn't tell me?" Mr. Kent's eyes cut deep into Clay's soul.

"Sir, it was not my secret to tell."

Around the Table

Chapter #11

Arthur Kent leaned back in his chair and crossed his arms.

Granny pushed her bowl of stew aside. She looked somewhere beyond Beep and whispered, "You knew last night Papa was dead, and you did not tell me."

"Granny, I didn't know how to tell you. I came in, and you were on the floor, and I didn't know how bad hurt you were. Then you got up early and left before I woke up. And I couldn't tell you while you were working. Besides, you always say that cooking soothes your soul."

A wisp of sorrow swept over Granny's face and settled in her eyes. A limp smile graced her lips. "Darlin', it be fine. I knew your papa was already with the Lord. The two of us have been one for years, and in my heart, I knew he was gone."

"Granny, … I am so sorry… Please don't be upset with me… I didn't know how to tell you… or… when to tell you… I just didn't know," Beep's shoulders shook, and sobs interrupted her speech.

"Darlin', I don't know if there is a right way or a wrong way to tell someone that the Half the Lord gave, the Lord took away. It was the good Lord's choice. He made that decision, and He will see us through. Now come and hug me, and know I am not upset with you, Darlin'."

Beep ran to her granny, and her granny scooped her into her lap. Beep was a big bundle, but there was no other place either wanted to be.

Clay ripped his eyes from the two and settled them on the floor. He didn't dare let Mr. Kent see him struggling with tears, and he thought God had just traded his pint-sized jar for a quart-sized jar.

Ole Honker slipped under the ladies' chair and lay his head on Granny's foot. Quietly, he moaned his sorrows for them.

Mr. Kent studied the scene without a word.

Finally, Beep sniffed, pulled away from Granny, and stood. "You are not upset?"

Granny dug in her apron pocket, dragged out a handkerchief, and used it wisely. "Darlin', I am not upset with you," she narrowed her eyes and stood, "but I do plan to meet Deputy Sneedle face-to-face."

Arthur Kent sat up, "Mrs. Johnston,"

Granny held up her hand to silence the man. "Mr. Kent, Deputy Sneedle killed my husband. I have every right to stand in front of him, point my finger in his face, and accuse him. I want to see his eyeballs when I tell him that I know what he did."

"Yes, Ma'am, you do have that right, but we need to talk about a few things first."

"Yes, we do. Mr. Kent, you said it looked like my Thomas had had a fishing accident. Why?" Granny's hands were fisted together.

"Mrs. Johnston, please, sit. I want you to understand that what we found was not pretty."

Granny placed her shaky hands on the edge of the table.

Beep made eye contact with Clay and nodded toward Granny's rocker.

Clay stepped over and carried the rocker to the table.

"Thank you, Clay." Granny switched from her chair and sat in her rocker with her head held high.

Beep tucked her knitted shawl about her shoulders. Then, the girl pulled a chair close, sat beside her granny, and held her hand.

Ole Honker squeezed between the two and settled with his head on his paws.

"Mr. Kent, you may begin," Granny, every bit a lady, told him.

"Would you like some hot tea or coffee?" he asked.

"Coffee would be nice. I always have some on the stove."

"I'll get it," Clay stepped over to the stove. He poured a steaming cup and brought it to the table.

"Thank you, Clay. There should be a plenty if you want a cup, too."

Clay smiled, "Thanks. Anybody else?"

Beep nodded.

"Please," Mr. Kent said.

When the coffee was delivered, and those few surrounded the table, Mr. Kent began. "Shall we ask the Lord to be the one in charge of our hearts?"

Granny's grief-stricken eyes traveled from the bolted doors to the dim light to behold the man across the table. "This must be how the disciples felt behind closed doors after their Lord Jesus was crucified."

The silence that followed was thick enough to cut with a knife. For the first time, Clay knew how those disciples were feeling without Jesus. They were without their closest friend and afraid the same men who took Jesus would come and drag them away to be crucified, too. Those same thoughts had been running rampant in his mind. His dad was gone. Would they try to come and take him, too?

Mr. Kent swallowed what sounded like a choking sob and dropped his head. "Yes, Ma'am. It must have been."

Clay knew. He was not the only one with a jar. God had a jar with Mr. Kent's name on it.

It was a bit before Mr. Kent could talk out loud, but finally, he started. "Lord, we are yours, and we thank you for it. Give us your strength to accept Bro. Thomas' death, and we thank you for the comfort of knowing he is in your arms. We ask for your wisdom to determine which steps we must take to bring the guilty to justice and protect the innocent. Again, thank you, Lord."

There wasn't a dry eye when they raised their heads, except for Ole Honker. He wolfed in his sleep.

Beep jumped and giggled.

The lamp light caught all the glassy, tear-filled eyes glittering with mirth. Clay was warmed with a homey kinship from those about the table.

Granny twisted the fringe from her shawl. "Mr. Kent, please tell me why you thought Thomas must have had a fishing accident."

Mr. Kent took a long pull of his coffee and began. "Mrs. Johnston, we did not find all of Thomas. We found parts of him in the river. He had a fishing vest on with several fishing hooks strung on a wire inside a pocket. A cane fishing pole was found on the bank close to the floating body."

Granny leaned over the table and rested her chin in her hands. She asked, "He didn't own a fishing vest, and the kids said he was shot between the eyes. How could you mistake that for a fishing accident?"

"Mrs. Johnston, I am sorry," he took a deep breath, "The body, Thomas' body, was found without a head."

No one said a word while their heartbeats rose to a crescendo.

"Without his head?" Beep's eyes were about to pop out of their sockets.

Clay shivered and swallowed a big lump in his throat. "No head?"

The color drained from Granny's face. "No head?" she whispered. Then she looked Mr. Kent straight in the eyes, "Why was I not asked to identify my husband's body? And where is his body now?"

Mr. Kent took a deep breath and shrugged, "Sheriff Millstrup had Deputy Sneedle put the…body in a coffin and transport it to the police lab in New Orleans."

"Without having me identify my own husband?"

"He told me he was trying to save you sorrow and grief, Ma'am."

Granny slapped the table, and everyone jumped. "That was wrong! He was my husband, and I have every right to make sure it was my husband."

"Ma'am, Mrs. Johnston, I agree completely with you, but it has already been done. Deputy Sneedle took the body to Monroe and put it on the afternoon train to New Orleans."

Granny stood and walked a circle around the table. "What if it was not my husband?"

Clay's eyes were wide. He wanted to tell her that even if it wasn't her husband, her husband was dead, and Granny gave him his chance.

Granny stopped and stood over Clay. "Young Man, is my husband dead?"

Shivers skedaddled over Clay. "Yes, Ma'am. He was dead. Beep and I would not have left him if he weren't dead."

"Thank you, Clay. Thank you for that."

Beep slipped beside her granny, "Please come and sit down."

Granny blindly followed Beep to the rocker and sat.

Quietly, Mr. Kent said, "Let's talk of the things that happened that we do know about. Maybe we can put all the events in order, as we would put together a puzzle.

All agreed.

"My first question is, why was your husband out on the river last night?"

Granny held her cup of coffee for warmth as she thought back to that night. "Thomas was worried. Men, his men working the pipeline, have disappeared, and some have been killed. Most of them are new to our Rocky Branch and have come here for jobs. Jobs have been hard to find, and they need the money. The pipeline has been a Godsend throughout this depression. Thomas noticed that those killed or those who had disappeared were newcomers to our area without families. He wondered why. He heard some men talking, and I think Thomas may have had an idea of what was happening and who was behind it. He heard someone mention a meeting. Thomas wanted to be in on that meeting, not so they would know he was there, but he wanted to hear what was going on and what was being planned."

"Did he name any names?"

Granny looked directly across the table at Mr. Kent. "He told me it would be better if I did not know. He said it was for my safety."

Mr. Kent narrowed his eyes, "Why in the world did he take your granddaughter?"

Granny set her coffee cup down, crossed her arms, and raised one eyebrow higher than the other, "Bee Poppy? I'll let you answer that question."

All eyes were on Beep.

She sat up straight in her chair. "He didn't. He told me I had to stay here, but I was worried about him. So, I waited to hear Granny snore, then I snuck out and followed him. I knew where he was going because I had listened to him tell Granny. By the time I caught up with him, it was too late for him to send me home."

"Was Deputy Sneedle alone?"

"'Puty Sneedle?"

Granny snapped her fingers. "Young Lady, that does not show respect. I don't know where you got that name, but…"

"He doesn't deserve respect. I watched him murder Papa. He gets no respect from me," Beep gasped.

Clay broke in, "I gave him that name, Ma'am. When we were in the Best Biscuits Around Café, I noticed the 'De' of deputy on his badge was covered… with…" he paused, not knowing how to tell this lady the deputy's badge had her husband's dried blood on it.

Beep finished the sentence for him, "The 'De' was covered in dried blood, and it was Papa's dried blood!"

Granny leaned back and closed her eyes, "That horrible man, that… that…horrible 'Puty Sneedle!"

Clay turned his head away from Granny because he thought he might laugh.

Beep did. "Granny, that does not show respect," she teased.

Granny turned slowly to Beep, "It certainly does not, and I'll answer for it when I meet my maker, but he will answer for what he did when he meets his maker. And I would like to help him step into that meeting." She looked toward the ceiling. "I would not want to be in his shoes."

Mr. Kent shook his head and chuckled. "Laughter in the midst of the storm. Isn't God good." He tapped the table, "I still have questions. Clay, what were you doing out on the river?"

"I was looking for my dad. He's been gone more than a week now."

With a wave of understanding and love, Granny gently placed her hand on his hand.

Mr. Kent closed his eyes for a moment, nodded, then continued, "How did you end up with Beep?"

Clay spoke slowly, "It was foggy, and I was in the middle of the river. A shot smashed on the left bank, and I figured I had better get out of there, so I pointed my boat to the right bank. Then I heard 'Puty Sneedle say, 'Girlie, you best come with me.' Then Beep started calling him a murderer, and I knew I couldn't leave a girl out in the swamp with a man who had just killed her papa. So, I rowed to the other bank, and Ole Honker and me? We took out looking for them. When we got close enough, I could see Beep's Papa had been shot between the eyes. Then 'Puty Sneedle tried to step over the dead body, and he tripped and fell. Somehow, his belly got caught in the dead man's arm, and it looked like Beep's Papa came alive and fought him. I thought 'Puty Sneedle was going crazy. Then Beep up and kicked 'Puty Sneedle in the head and ran. That is what saved her life because it looked like and sounded like he was going to kill her, too."

Granny was holding her breath.

Mr. Kent was tapping his fingers on the tabletop.

"This is not good." Mr. Kent pressed his lips together.

A long silence followed.

Clay licked his lips. "There is more."

Mr. Kent looked at him, "More? Well, let's have it."

Clay pulled out the note they had found in the tree from his pocket, laid it on the table, and ironed it flat with his hand. "Beep," he nodded at her.

She took her Papa's glove and placed it beside the note.

Granny gasped, "Thomas' glove." Lovingly, she pulled it close. She felt something inside the glove and held it upside-down. Coins dropped, sounding like rich hailstones: hard, cold, and destructive.

Clay tapped the note on the table and looked from Granny directly at Mr. Kent. "'Puty Sneedle was paid to kill Beep's Papa."

A Shot in the Night

'In the Sweet By and By

Chapter #12

It was agreed that Beep and Clay lay low for a few days. What 'Puty Sneedle did not see, he would not think about. But it had been three days of 'laying low' now. Clay walked around the inside of the cabin again, looking out each window as he passed it. It was as if the outside called to him.

Ole Honker followed Clay and protested with an antsy yelp. He wanted to run, and he needed to run. He was a good-sized hunting dog, and there was nothing to hunt in the cabin except maybe a mouse. But even the mice seem to stay clear of Ole Honker.

"I'm sorry, Ole Boy. I'm just following orders for 'safety's sake.' That is what Mr. Kent called it." Clay sat on his cot and rubbed his dog's belly.

Mr. Kent had sent a few messages, and today he had some leads to check on. Despite Clay's begging, Mr. Kent would not budge enough to let Clay go with him; instead, he told Clay to stay put in the cabin and keep watch until he returned.

But Clay was as stir-crazy as Ole Honker. Nothing moved outside besides birds, frogs, and squirrels, and Ole Honker wanted to chase them all. Besides, Clay figured 'Puty Sneedle would not be back here. He had already searched the cabin and found nothing he could use. Clay rubbed his head.

He had to get out of this place, and he wanted to see Beep. He needed to see Beep.

"Ole Honker, we need a walk," he scruffed the dog's neck.

Ole Honker yapped and threw his back end into a tailspin.

Clay stood and patted the handgun stuck in the back of his trouser waistband. He didn't have any bullets besides the ones it already held. His dad should have had some, but he hadn't found them, and he had looked. He plopped his hat on his head and walked toward the door.

Ole Honker was already there, standing on his hind legs and scratching the door with his paws.

"I know, Ole Honker. We have got to get out of here. Want to go check on Beep?" Clay cracked the door to check outside.

Ole Honker yelped a "Yes!" and shoved his nose into the crack and pushed the door wide.

A blue jay scolded, but Ole Honker didn't care. He tore away from the cabin.

"Wait up, Ole Boy," Clay called. But Ole Honker had his front paws on the side of a tree trunk, barking at a squirrel flitting from branch to branch.

Clay shook his head and grinned, remembering the squirrel in the black gum tree who now sported a bent, broken tail. "You'd think a dog would learn what damage a squirrel can do to him."

The afternoon sun stretched her sun rays like fingers, searching the deep shadows of the trees. She was trying to find cool spots and warm them up, and she was doing a good job of it. Clay pulled his hat from his head and wiped the sweat off his forehead. He looked through the trees and up to the sky. It was good to be outside.

He did not walk the trail to Rocky Branch. He stayed a few feet deep into the edge of the trees and stepped quietly.

Ole Honker bounded from one side of him to the other, and Clay did not have the heart to slow him down. Being cooped up was not the dream of a hound dog.

At the edge of Rocky Branch, Clay stopped to study the streets. There were automobiles lined up on both sides of the main street. And plenty of people were browsing the boardwalks. He decided it would be better to trust the alleys. He waited until everyone seemed to be occupied with their errands, warned Ole Honker to be quiet, pulled his hat low over his eyes, and stepped into the street. His heart pounded. He had walked these streets so many times with no fear. Now, he trusted no one. He slipped into the first alley he came to and thought it was the alley behind the main street. That would be the alley that went right behind The Best Biscuit Around Café. "Good," he whispered, then he groaned as he studied the alley. Every single establishment had a back door that could open at any time right into his path. He sighed. He could not afford to get caught, but he needed to see Beep. He had to tackle the alley. He stuck his hands in his pockets and started. He hardly breathed because all the businesses had their windows open. The only good thing was that the noise from inside helped drown out his footsteps.

Halfway through the alley, Ole Honker stopped to sniff about the steps of an establishment. He pointed with his nose and tail. Clay stopped and watched as Ole Honker's body vibrated with a low growl.

Clay watched the hair on the back of Ole Honker's neck prickle to a stand. A shiver crawled up Clay's spine. He froze. He swallowed and looked up. The sign read: Sheriff's Office.

Quickly, he reached down to shush Ole Clay and heard Sheriff Millstrup's gravelly voice. "I told you to take care of things."

"Boss, I did the best I could."

Clay pressed his back against the building. That voice belonged to 'Puty Sneedle. He would know it anywhere, and he wanted to hear every word. He knelt beside Ole Honker and gently closed his hands about his nose and whispered, "Quiet." Then he inched to the window and peeked inside.

"That was the best you could do?" Sheriff Millstrup was mad. "Do you know what I thought when the crew dragged in chunks of old man Johnston?"

"No, Sir." 'Puty Sneedle's voice was shaking.

"I thought it would have been better if it had been chunks of you. When I pay a man, I expect him to do the job I pay him for, and I expect him to clean up after himself." He pounded on the top of his desk.

Clay thought the whole building shook, and 'Puty Sneedle must have thought the same thing. He jumped and tried to swallow a girlie scream.

Sheriff Millstrup exploded into a stand, scooting his chair across the wooden floorboards.

'Puty Sneedle's face drained beneath his patchy whiskers.

Sheriff Millstrup pulled in a deep breath and rubbed his forehead. "Sit down, Sneedle."

'Puty Sneedle sat.

"Did you get the body to the train?" Sheriff Millstrup pointed.

"Yes, Sir. Just like you told me. I drove it in the hearse all the way to Monroe and had it loaded on the train."

"Did you check the body?"

He nodded, "Boss, I made sure nothin' could come back on us. The bullet was in the head and," he swallowed, "there ain't a head no more. I made sure it was gone."

"You cut off his head?" Sheriff Millstrup squinted in disgust.

"Boss," he spread his hands, "I was trying to make it look like a fishin' accident. I put my old fishing vest with some fishin' hooks in the pockets on his body. I left a fishin' pole on the bank, where I dragged him to the river. And I dropped him in the water so the blood would gather the gators, and it would look like the gators got a hold of him."

"Good." Sheriff Millstrup paused, "I suppose it will work." The sheriff rubbed his hands together in thought. He turned back to 'Puty Sneedle. "Now for the girl. She saw you?"

'Puty Sneedle nodded.

"Then she can identify you. She has got to go."

'Puty Sneedle clamped his hands on the sides of the chair. "How do you mean 'go'?"

Sheriff Millstrup sat, leaned over the papers on his desk, and eyeballed the man. "The same way her papa went, Sneedle. Kill her."

Clay watched 'Puty Sneedle's Adam's apple bob up and down, and slowly, he licked his chapped lips, "A… Boss… She's only a girl."

The boss grinned, "Why so she is, and when she tells me, the sheriff, that you are the one who shot her papa, I am going to put you in handcuffs, throw you in my jail cell, and slam the door. Then there will be a trial, and everyone will believe that sweet, innocent, little girl. You will be found guilty, and you will be sentenced to hang by the neck until dead. Do you understand that 'Puty Sneedle?"

A wild glaze covered 'Puty Sneedle's eyes as he realized he would hang. He nodded. His eyes glinted with a faraway sheen, and he glared before he whispered, "You called me 'Puty. I don't like that, Boss."

At the window, Clay felt like he had been punched in the stomach. He had thought 'Puty Sneedle was scared. Now, he knew he was more than scared. He was crazy. Clay remembered his dad warning him, "Son if you suspect a man of not being in his right mind, get away from him as fast as you can because he can't be reasoned with." Clay could feel it in his bones. 'Puty Sneedle was not a sane man. He was a crazy man.

Sheriff Millstrup leaned back in his chair. "I am your boss, Sneedle. I will call you as I wish, and you have earned that name. You had the blood of the man you murdered on your badge, and you got caught with it. That was sloppy, 'Puty. If it were tested…" he let it hang in the air.

'Puty Sneedle nibbled his bottom lip. "I scrubbed it off my badge."

Sheriff Millstrup studied the man before he spoke, "'Puty, go do your job."

Slowly, 'Puty Sneedle stood and walked toward the door.

Sheriff Millstrup stopped him, "Not the front door, 'Puty. Go out the back door."

"Not good enough for the front door, huh?" 'Puty Sneedle whispered as he turned to face the sheriff.

Clay wildly looked for a place to hide. The trash cans were close, so he dove in headfirst and then thought of the noise he had made. "Stupid mistake," he groaned.

'Puty Sneedle was so rankled that he slammed the door, stomped down the steps, and kicked at Old Honker, who hadn't known to move out of sight.

Old Honker skedaddled, yelping across the alley and between the buildings.

'Puty Sneedle shoved his hands in his pocket and began whistling, 'In the Sweet By and By.'

Clay's heartbeat was drumming against the side of the trash barrel in time with the insane man and his tune, 'In the Sweet By and By.'

With One Stone

Chapter #13

Clay hunched in the trash can until he knew 'Puty Sneedle was out of sight. Slowly, he topped his eyes over the edge. 'Puty Sneedle was long gone, but so was Ole Honker. Clay didn't dare whistle for his dog. He didn't want Sheriff Millstrup to find him. Quietly, Clay stood and brushed off his clothes. He was glad it wasn't the trash behind The Best Biscuits Around Café. That would take more than just brushing. He stepped out of the can and looked up and down the alley. He needed to find Beep. He wasn't too worried about Ole Honker. He could take care of himself, and he knew Ole Honker would find him. But Beep was another story. She had to be protected, and he hoped Mr. Kent would come back soon. He would know what to do.

'Puty Sneedle had been gone long enough now, and Clay was far enough away from the sheriff's office that he whistled for Ole Honker, but Ole Honker didn't come. His dog sure must be exploring streets further away in Rocky Branch. Hopefully, he remembered the trash can in the alley of the Best Biscuits Around Café. Clay tucked his hands in his pockets and strode down the alley. He headed straight for The Best Biscuits Around Café. He was counting on Beep working there with her granny, and that worried him since 'Puty Sneedle was looking for her, and 'Puty Sneedle always ate at Granny's café.

He turned into the side alley and laughed. Ole Honker was sitting and whining at the café's screen door. Beep stepped out and looked about. She didn't see a soul, so she bent to hug the dog. Ole Honker lapped at her cheek and wiggled his tail. Clay sighed. He knew it. He was going to lose his best friend to a girl.

Beep looked up and saw Clay, "I thought you must be close by. The two of you always travel together. Come on in."

"Gladly." The kitchen aromas wafted through the air, and his stomach rumbled.

Beep scrunched her eyes, "I heard that. Are you always hungry?"

He shrugged, "Your Granny said it. I can't help it. I'm a growing boy."

Beep shook her head, "Well, come on in." She opened the door for Clay, but Ole Honker nosed in front of the boy and tried to squeeze through.

"Oh, no, you don't," Granny grabbed the broom to block the threshold. "You know the rules. No dogs in my kitchen." Then she turned to Beep and whispered so no one else could hear, "The Young Missy out in the dining room did not clean her plate. I just brought it back to the kitchen. Take it out and scrape it for Ole Honker."

"Yes, Ma'am." Beep took the plate with a smile, stepped out the door, and Ole Honker moaned as if he knew he would have a taste of heaven.

Clay told his dog to stay and eased into the kitchen. He had to let Granny and Beep know that 'Puty Sneedle was going to try to kill Beep, and Clay knew he wouldn't stop at killing Beep. Granny was in danger, too.

"Wash those hands, Bee Poppy," Granny said. "I heard the bell jingle, so we have another customer."

"Yes, Ma'am." Beep went to the sink and rinsed her hands. She dried them and headed to the swinging kitchen doors. She stepped out, paused for a second, whipped around, and scurried back into the kitchen again. She was white when she turned to face them. "'Puty Sneedle is our new customer. Granny, I don't trust him, but I'll take him a cup of coffee." She hesitated and grinned, "Do you have arsenic for his coffee?"

Granny's lips were in a grim line, "Not today, but I can get some." She stepped to the doors and looked over them, studying 'Puty Sneedle.

Clay had to stop Beep before 'Puty Sneedle laid his mangy eyes on her. He spoke low and fast, "Beep, you can't go out there. He is planning to kill you. I heard Sheriff Millstrup and him talking. The sheriff told him to get rid of you because you can identify him."

Beep was wide-eyed. She wrapped her arms about herself and shook as if she were freezing. "I knew it. That night, I knew he wanted me dead. That is why I ran off and left Papa. It figures that he still wants me dead."

Granny stood tall and took a deep breath. "Dead? We will see about that, and I promise I will not let that man lay a hand on you. You can mark my words." She pulled the towel from her shoulder and tossed it over her arm. "I will personally take care of this customer."

"You can't. If he knows you are Beep's Granny, he'll kill you, too," Clay told her.

"'Puty Sneedle? He does not know me. He comes in here every day, and every day, he looks down on me as if I am beneath him. He probably won't even look at me when he gives me his order. But," she held up her finger, "I know him." Granny stepped out of the swinging doors as if she were the queen of the world.

Clay watched from the slit in the swinging doors. Granny seemed to swoop over to the table in the corner facing the door, where 'Puty Sneedle liked to sit, and asked what he wanted to order. Granny was right. He had a newspaper and never even looked up from it.

"The special," he told her.

"Yes, Sir." She scribbled something on the order book she had and shoved it into her apron pocket. "It will be out shortly."

"Good," he said from behind the paper. "And I'll take coffee now."

Granny pressed her lips together, cleared her throat, and nodded. "Right up."

Clay noticed Granny did not say a 'yes, sir,' and he thought it was a godsend that 'Puty Sneedle never looked from his paper to Granny because he surely would have seen death in her eyes.

As she went back to the kitchen, Janet, the mayor's wife, stopped her. "Ouida, are you well?"

Granny stood silent. She couldn't say a word, not with 'Puty Sneedle in earshot, and a flood of feelings had busted out of her heart where she had kept them locked. As far as she knew, the identity of the man who had been found in the fishing accident had not been announced, but then, how could they? He had no head.

Janet rose and put her arm about Granny. "How can I help?"

Granny shook her head. "It's just a bit of a headache. It will pass, and I will be fine. Mrs. Shay, if you want to help, I know you to be a praying woman. Please, say a prayer for me and mine."

"Of course, Ouida, but if you would let me, I would close the kitchen for you so you could leave early. You could go home, rest, and take care of that headache."

Granny smiled. Janet was one of those ladies who didn't care who you married, what job you held, or what color your skin was. What she felt came from the heart, and Janet left God to be the judge of her heart. "Thank you, Mrs. Shay. I will leave things in the Almighty's hands. He'll take care of me and mine." Granny spoke loud enough that all in her café could hear if they listened. She did not figure it would make a dent in the heart of 'Puty Sneedle, but her God was a God of miracles.

Janet's lips smiled, but her eyes held concern. "If there is anything I can do, you will let me know?"

"Yes, Ma'am, Mrs. Shay."

"Janet. Call me Janet. We are friends, and I would love for you to call me Janet."

Granny thrashed through the worry and found a smile that calmed her nerves. "Janet, it is then."

Granny swooshed through the swinging doors and found a wall to lean against. She looked past the ceiling and spoke, "Lord, you are going to have to help me. He killed my Thomas, and he wants to kill my Bee Poppy, and I need to take a plate to the man. If I had that arsenic, Lord, I would love to give him a mighty big dose. But…I guess I will have to leave it up to you."

Clay crossed to Granny. "Ma'am, I can take the plate out there, so you won't have to look at him again. I don't think he saw me the other night, not face-to-face. It was dark, and we were running." It was not a lie. 'Puty Sneedle could not have known him from that night, but after eating breakfast with 'Puty Sneedle the next morning, the man was bound to remember him. Yet Granny did not know that, and Clay did not want her to have to stand in his presence again.

Granny was quiet. "I can't push off my job on a boy."

Clay grinned as he pressed to persuade her, "You call me a young man."

Granny shook her head, "Out of the mouth of babes…"

Clay pushed harder, "Besides, you said so yourself: he won't look up from his paper to see who is bringing his food."

Granny had been too mad to cry. But this boy was giving his all to protect her, and he was just a boy. She shook her head. King David had been just a boy when he killed Goliath with one stone, and God called him a man after his own heart. Had God sent her a boy to kill a giant? Now tears were making rivers down the age-worn lines of her face. She pulled the hem of her apron to her face and tried to dam up the tears. "You are a good young man, Clay, and I believe I will take you up on that offer. The special is on the stove, poor man's shepherd's pie, and biscuits."

"Yes, Ma'am." Clay took a plate and went to the stove.

Beep stepped behind him with a glint in her eye. "Clay, we could spit in it."

Clay laughed.

"No, you will not, Young Lady. We do not spit in anyone's food, even if they are an enemy," Granny hissed.

Beep whirled around to face her Granny, her eyes sparked with fire, "But he cut off Papa's head!"

"Yes, he did, and he will pay for it. God will take care of him and do a better job of it than we ever could." Granny left no room for argument.

Beep dropped her head. "Yes, Ma'am."

Clay had seen Beep's face. If Granny had not stood to watch, he figured that 'Puty Sneedle would have had a very 'spicy' load of shepherd's pie. He took the plate and headed for the swinging doors.

Just as he placed the plate in front of 'Puty Sneedle, Mr. Kent pulled out a chair and sat across from the Deputy.

Caught! But Mr. Kent did not say a word; yet Clay knew he had seen him. He was like his dad. He never missed anything.

With a fleeting glance, Mr. Kent's eyes told him they would talk later. He then turned to 'Puty Sneedle, "Deputy, we had breakfast together a few days ago. It was so enjoyable, I thought I would join you again."

'Puty Sneedle glared at the man. "I remember."

"Good. I thought we might chat about that case you have. You know the case of the man killed in the fishing accident."

One side of the deputy's mouth turned up in a sneer, "Mister, we don't discuss our cases with just anyone. It would be unprofessional. So, if you will excuse me, I would rather eat alone. I have a lot on my mind."

Mr. Kent chuckled, and his eyes twinkled. "I'll bet you do have a lot on your mind."

"What does that mean?" 'Puty Sneedle growled.

Mr. Kent thumped the table, "It's a big case. That means there is much to think about, maybe a lot of loose ends?"

"Puty Sneedle narrowed his eyes. "Loose ends?"

Mr. Kent nodded and grinned, "I want to hear all you know, and I have a few questions myself."

'Puty Sneedle yanked his gun out of his holster and dropped it on the table. "Mr., I don't want to eat with you, so you can get yourself up and out of here right now. We don't talk about our cases over dinner or any other time. It is a matter of privacy, and it is none of your business. Now get out of here before I arrest you."

Everyone in the café had stopped eating.

Clay had stopped breathing.

Mr. Kent leaned back in his chair and chuckled. "Oh, Deputy, I think you will want to talk to me."

'Puty Sneedle jerked himself from his chair to stand over Mr. Kent, "Get out!" He pointed to the door.

"Not this time, Deputy Sneedle." Slowly, Mr. Kent reached into his inside coat pocket and pulled out a square piece of leather. He flipped it open and boldly dropped it on the table. The sound was as if a stone had hit its mark. When it settled, it displayed a shiny badge embossed with the U.S. Marshal label.

'Puty Sneedle gasped as if the stone had hit him. His shoulders sagged, and his knees felt as if they would give way.

Mr. Kent looked up at the man with a lop-sided grin, "U.S. Marshal Kent at your service, and I hope you will be at my service, too. Now, have a seat, Deputy Sneedle. We have much to talk about."

A Gallon Jar

Chapter #14

Evening shadows were falling, and Clay hated them. He was glad that it meant the air was cooling, but it also meant the dark was slipping in like the boogie man. He was almost to his cabin, but he was alone. Ole Honker was with Beep, and he was thankful. Beep and Granny needed the protection the old hound would give, but it made him feel naked and alone. Alone was not the best idea after knowing what 'Puty Sneedle had done to Beep's Papa, and now Clay knew Sheriff Millstrup was just as bad, if not worse.

Clay stayed in the shadows of the forest, with the squirrels scolding him every step. At the edge of the cabin clearing, Clay stopped. He remembered the last time he had come home, and the door had been jarred open, but then he had not been alone. Marshal Kent had been with him. Now, he was alone and wished for the Marshal. Wishes were like stars. They are the beauty of the night, but you must wait to catch a falling star to make your wish, and you could wait a lifetime to catch a falling star. His mom had told him that, and she said prayers work much better than wishes. He shook the warm memory away to study the cabin.

The door was shut, but still, he waited and listened. He had to because Ole Clay wasn't there to do it for him. Nothing. There was no movement or sound. He inched closer and decided to follow the trees around the cabin, making a circle of the area. By the time he was done making his circle, the stars were fighting to shine. He needed to hurry.

From the side of the cabin, he stepped onto the porch. Those weathered floorboards creaked with every step; so much for being unannounced. He crossed through the door and gritted his teeth. He had waited too long. Now, he would have to light a lantern. He could do it in the dark if the lantern was where it was supposed to be. It was. He sighed with relief. Mr. Kent, no, Marshal Kent, he corrected himself, needed the duffle he had stowed beneath the floorboards under Clay's bed. Clay had been surprised when Marshal Kent told him about the hideaway hole. It was under his bed, and how long had he slept over that hideaway and never known it existed?

Clay found the matches and tried to strike one, but he was shaking and fumbled with the match. He was disgusted with himself. He tried again but had the same luck. "Forget the match," he threw it on the floorboards and stepped on it. Maybe it would be better to find the duffle in the dark. He knew where his bunk was, and Marshal Kent had drawn a map of the hideaway in the dirt outside of Beep's home, so he knew where the hideaway hole was. Carefully, he crossed to his bunk and sank to his knees. He stuck his head under the bed and felt for the seams of the hideaway hole. There it was. He traced the seams with his finger, and it was just like the map Marshal Kent had drawn. It was not square. It was three boards across, but each plank of the lid was a different length, cut from the floorboards. It blended in with the floorboards so well that it completely disguised the hole. No wonder he had never noticed that space before. He reached into his pocket and took out his pocketknife to pry the top off the hideaway hole. He felt inside the hole, found the duffle, pulled it out, and tossed it on top of his bunk. Carefully, he placed the lid back on the hideaway hole and smiled. He would use that later when things got back to normal, if they ever got back to normal.

Clay took the duffle and stood. Now, he could get out of here. It was eerie alone, in the night, after the murder of Beep's Papa and the disappearance of his dad. Marshal Kent had planned for them to meet at Granny's cabin, and Clay was ready to get there. There was comfort in being with those you trusted.

Clay took a step toward the door and stopped. What was that? He heard it again, and it made his skin crawl. Something was out there. An animal? Clay wished for his dog. It felt like the hairs on the back of his neck had risen to attention just as they did on Ole Honker when danger was in the air. He froze to listen, his heart pounding. There it was again.

"I tell you, I searched the place, and there wasn't anything there."

Clay rolled his eyes. It was 'Puty Sneedle, and he was not alone.

Clay gasped. He had to get out of here, and he had to do it now. He could not be caught by 'Puty Sneedle.

"Well, 'Puty, you told me you almost got caught and had to jump out the window, so I figure you must have missed something. It's got to be there."

And that voice belonged to Sheriff Millstrup. Clay began to sweat. He knew he was in trouble. The only way out besides the door was through the broken window. And that would make noise.

"But, Boss," 'Puty Sneedle began.

"'Puty, quit your bellyaching and get in there," Sheriff Millstrup ordered.

There was a long pause, followed by angry muttering. Then Clay heard 'Puty on the steps, and chills traveled over his spine. He jumped onto his bunk, and the springs groaned and whined. He didn't wait to see if he had been heard. He grabbed the duffle, threw it out the window, and followed suit.

"Someone's in there," 'Puty Sneedle yelled and rushed across the porch. It was dark in the cabin, and he stopped at the door.

Clay picked up a rock and threw it through the window just as a breeze caught the curtain in a dance. Then, he smashed his body against the logs and snaked his way to the edge of the cabin. He took a deep breath and peeked around the edge.

The rock had worked.

'Puty Sneedle jumped, screamed, ran, and smashed into a porch pole. He fell back, scrambled to his knees, and wildly crawled to torpedo through Sheriff Millstrup's legs. Together, they rolled and splashed on the ground like a gallon of spilled paint.

Clay's heart raced, and his legs followed. He disappeared into the forest before the glob of Sneedle and Millstrup could get untangled. All the while, 'Puty Sneedle shouted about haunts, and Sheriff Millstrup yelled in a not-so-nice language about useless deputies. The last thing he bellowed was, "There is no such thing as a haunt, Sneedle. Be a man. Maybe it was a bear, but it was not a haunt."

"A bear? You didn't see that curtain reaching to grab me!"

When Clay was out of earshot, he doubled over with laughter. What he had seen would be branded in his mind forever, but what he knew the Lord had saved him from would be one of the treasures he would carry all his life.

He slowed down. The woods were dark, and he did not trust the path. Sure, Puty Sneedle and Sheriff Millstrup were not in town, but they had others working for them, and he did not know who they were. The pistol in his waistband was witness to that. How many were there anyway, and why? What did they want? Maybe Marshal Kent would know.

At the edge of town, he stopped to look before he stepped into the street. It was safe so far as he could tell, and it was a relief to know that Sheriff

Millstrup and 'Puty Sneedle would be busy searching his cabin for a while.

Clay crossed the main street and took the alley to Beep's house. He didn't have to knock on the door because Ole Honker started howling a welcome. Marshal Kent opened the door. "I was getting worried, Clay." He pulled the boy inside, shut, and bolted the door.

Clay nodded. "I had visitors."

"I was afraid you might. Who?"

"'Puty Sneedle and Sheriff Millstrup. They are in this together."

Marshal Kent's eyes were knowing. "I thought so. Did they see you?"

Clay shook his head. "Almost. I jumped out of the window, which 'Puty Sneedle jumped through the other day. I threw a rock through the window, and somehow, it scared the fire out of 'Puty Sneedle. He tore out of there, screaming about haunts. He knocked the sheriff over, and I ran." He tipped his head, and as the thought hit him, he said, "I don't think 'Puty Sneedle is right in his head."

Marshal Kent crossed his arms and tapped his fingers on his biceps. "He is not 'right in the head', and I want you to remember that because it makes him a very dangerous man. He is not afraid of anything."

"Except haunts," Clay said.

Marshal Kent nodded. "That is something to remember. We might be able to use it."

They sat around the table and ate leftovers from the café. Clay never flinched at a leftover. If it was good the first time, it was good the second time, and sometimes even better. Shepherd's pie with biscuits had been today's special, and it was good. Clay didn't waste time talking. He ate. Finally, he sat back in his chair and stifled a burp.

Granny raised her eyebrows. "I take that as a compliment?" she asked.

Everyone but Clay laughed.

The boy looked around the table, wondering what was so funny.

Beep told him. "The belch!"

Clay squinted, "You heard that?"

"They probably heard that belch in Ten Buck Two!" Beep giggled.

Again, laughter filled the air.

Clay gallantly stood and bowed. "You are welcome, and yes, it was a compliment, Mrs. Johnston."

Granny wiped a laughing tear from her cheek and paused long enough to say, "Clay, you may as well call me Granny. It will be easier for everyone concerned."

"Really? Granny? You mean it?" Clay had never known a grandmother or a grandfather, and it made his heart full and warm.

Granny nodded. "I sure do. Try it out, Young Man."

He looked around the table. Beep was all smiles. Marshal Kent sat back, pleased, and Granny clasped her hands in excitement.

Beep's Granny wanted him to call her Granny? She wanted to be his granny? Warmth spread over him. Well, that was a falling star he could catch and tuck in his heart. Clay took a moment to swallow those tears that seemed to be building. Before he knew it, God would have a gallon jar waiting to catch his tears. He looked into the face of Beep's granny. Her dark eyes held life, and crow's feet had left their tracks behind, but they were laughter trails. Her dark skin was soft, and her lips were full. Gray hair splayed, forming a halo about her head. Clay dragged his fingers through his hair to straighten it a bit. He tipped his head slightly, smiled, and whispered, "Granny."

The silence was sweet music around the table, and the song it sang was of the taste of a welcome home.

Granny put her hands on the edge of the table and pushed up, so she could stand. She crossed to the boy and wrapped her arms around him. "Oh, God, be so good. He give me the desires of my heart. I craved more than one grandchild, and he done give me two, a beautiful girl and now a fine-looking young man."

He was Elected

Chapter #15

Ole Honker raised his head and gave a deep, guttural growl.

No one moved, and all watched as someone tried to raise the latch on the door. Then someone leaned against the door, grunted, and shoved.

Marshal Kent put his finger to his lips for silence and shook his head. Then he mouthed the words, "Beep, Clay, hide."

Without sound, they climbed the ladder to the loft.

Granny caught on quickly. She gathered the bowls and cups from their places at the table and doused them in her dishpan of sudsy water.

The silence was split open by pounding on the door. Whoever was there had no patience. "Open up. We need to talk."

Even though it was outside the door and the night was deep, they all heard a deadly voice whisper, "I want that girl. We need that girl."

Ole Honker moved to the door.

"'Puty, keep a tight lip, will you?"

Granny looked at Marshal Kent.

His gaze traveled over the room, looking for a sign that the kids had been there; when he found none and felt they would be safe, he nodded an 'ok' for the door to be opened.

"Hold your horses," Granny called. "It's been a long day, and I am not as young as I used to be." She looked to Marshal Kent as she slowly walked toward the intrusion. At Marshal Kent's go-ahead, she unlatched the deadbolt and cracked the door, "Now, what is so all-fired important that it can't wait until morning?"

Ole Honker stuck his nose through the crack and growled.

Sheriff Millstrup took a step backward before he asked, "Ma'am, are you the lady who works at The Best Biscuits Around Café?" His voice was cold and hard.

"I am, and who might I be talking with?"

"I am the sheriff of Rocky Branch, Ma'am, and I have with me my deputy, Irwin Sneedle. We have gotten information that you work for The Best Biscuits Around Café. We are looking for a young girl who some have seen in your café. They even thought she might work with you in the café, and we have a few questions we would like to ask her.

Again, Granny looked at Marshal Kent, who nodded.

Granny edged the door open a might more and had her say. "I guess you may as well come on in, gentlemen, and I hesitate to call you gentlemen. I watched you try the door latch before you ever knocked, and I heard you bust against the door to spring it open. Given the law, I think you're acting very shady. And I tell you right now, I doubt I will trust you."

Sheriff Millstrup held up his hand, "Mrs. Johnston, let me explain. We heard no sounds of life, and I worried that evil had come upon you."

"Evil? I wonder why?" She looked them up and down. "Come on in, Sheriff, Deputy, and have a place at my table. I'll get you some coffee."

The men looked at the dog.

Granny grinned, "Move out of the way, Dog, but you keep your eyes on them shady lawmen."

Ole Honker sat beside Granny with the sides of his lips held up on his fang teeth. Granny smiled, "Good dog," she said.

The men stepped around the unfriendly dog and turned to the table. They saw Marshal Kent and stopped in their tracks.

"I don't like that none," 'Puty Sneedle mumbled and pointed a thumb at the Marshal.

"Shut it up," Sheriff Millstrup growled at his deputy.

Granny smiled, "I figured you boys might know each other, being how you are on the same side of the law. Sit down and get better acquainted."

Without taking their eyes off the Marshal, the two men walked to the table, pulled out chairs, and sat.

Granny brought cups of coffee and placed them down in front of the two men.

From above, Beep mouthed to Clay, "I wonder if Granny got that arsenic?"

Clay grinned, "I wish."

Granny refilled Marshal Kent's cup and then hers. She sat and dipped a heaping teaspoon of sweet grains from the sugar bowl and stirred them in.

Ole Honker moseyed over to Granny's chair and lay down between her and the two lawmen.

Granny put the spoon down and studied the two men. "Gentlemen, what do you need from an old woman?"

"Ma'am, we are looking for a young girl. We suspect she was involved in the disappearance of a man working on the pipeline, or that she has pertinent information regarding the disappearance. We know there was a dispute between the man and my deputy. The girl got away, and we would like to question her. Some said she may be the girl who works at The Best Biscuits Around Café. You are the cook there, aren't you?"

Granny narrowed her eyes. "I am the cook, the custodian, and the owner of that café."

"You own that place?" 'Puty Sneedle was shocked, and it showed.

"Yes, I do, even if I am a woman and a 'darkie' woman at that. Of course, my husband, George Washington Johnston, is my co-owner."

"Who?" 'Puty Sneedle's voice jumped an octave. "Johnston? He had a wife?" 'Puty Sneedle gulped, and his Adam's apple bobbed up and down.

Sheriff Millstrup smashed 'Puty's toe under the table.

"Ow!" 'Puty yelped. "What was that for?"

Granny glared, "Had? George Washington Johnston had a wife? What do you mean by 'had'? Is there something you need to tell me about my husband?"

"Nope. We only want to know about that girl, if she works for you, a… at the café, Ma'am," 'Puty Sneedle stumbled through the sentence. "We need to talk to her."

Granny narrowed her eyes, "Deputy, you come to my café every day I am open. If she worked there, surely, you would have seen her."

'Puty Sneedle blinked and shook his head. "I ain't seen her at the café. I ain't seen her around town. I don't know where she come from."

"But you have seen her? Where would that have been?" Granny narrowed her eyes as she asked.

'Puty Sneedle flushed, "I…I…I am the one asking the questions." He stood and pointed a bony finger at the lady. "We need to know where she is, and we think you know, and you better tell us. Where is she?"

"Why? You yourself said you had never seen her in my café. Why would you think I have seen her?"

'Puty Sneedle shook, "We need to find her, and I think you know where she is."

Sheriff Millstrup stood and placed his hand on 'Puty Sneedle's shoulder. "Calm down, Deputy." Then the sheriff directed his conversation to Mrs. Johnston. "Ma'am, this is my deputy's first murder case…"

"Murder?" Granny gasped.

"Yes, ma'am, murder. My deputy is a little wound up. Please excuse him." He turned to 'Puty Sneedle, "Go wait outside, Deputy."

'Puty Sneedle glared and stomped out, leaving the door ajar behind him.

Sheriff Millstrup shook his head. "He was elected. I did not choose him."

'Puty Sneedle slammed the door.

Sheriff Millstrup smacked his fist into the palm of his other hand and shook his head toward the door. "I apologize for my deputy, and I will have a talk with him." He gritted his teeth.

Granny nodded, "You had better do it soon. The Holy Book says, 'Make no friendship with an angry man; and with a furious man thou shalt not go: Lest thou learn his ways, and get a snare to thy soul.' That means his temper might rub off on you."

Sheriff Millstrup stood straight and stiff as his temper flared. He was the sheriff, and this woman had just scolded him. His face turned bright red, and fire shot from his eyes. He took a deep breath to calm down before he spoke, "Mrs. Johnston, if you know who and where the girl is, you need to tell us. She is wanted for questioning, and some even suspect she may have killed the man. Since that man was your husband, I would think you should want us to find her." Slowly, the sheriff placed his hands on the table and leaned in toward Granny. "Ma'am, if you know where she is, or who she is, it would be in your best interest to tell us."

Granny was shaking.

Ole Honker was snarling.

Sheriff Millstrup stepped back.

Marshal Kent cleared his throat and stood. "I am U.S. Marshal Arthur Kent, and, Sheriff, I rather think you have threatened this lady enough for one evening."

Sheriff Millstrup stood to his full height, "Marshal, maybe you didn't hear, this is a murder case, and this young girl is a suspect. I have every right to search this house now." He snapped his fingers and called, "Deputy Sneedle, I need you here front and center. We are going to search."

Deputy Sneedle sauntered through the doorway, "Reporting for duty, Sheriff."

"Search every inch of this place, and if we don't find that girl here, we'll go to the café and tear it apart."

Marshal Kent's jaw was tight. "Do you have a search warrant from the county judge?"

The sheriff's face turned a shade redder with anger. "I am the sheriff of this town."

"Then, as an officer of the law, you, of all people, know that you must have a search warrant for this to be legal. I will be here with Mrs. Johnston until you come back with one," Marshal Kent had his fingers hooked in his gun belt.

Ole Honker was ready to leap.

The sheriff pointed at the Marshal, "I will be back, and that is a promise. And… I will leave my deputy on duty outside this door." He slammed his hat on his head and almost ran out the door.

From outside, they heard him order 'Puty Sneedle, "No one goes in, and no one gets out."

Ole Honker howled, giving a warning that no one was welcome inside the door.

They heard Sheriff Millstrup scuff across the swept yard and slam the gate, and they figured 'Puty Sneedle sat and leaned against the door.

Ole Honker placed his nose on the door jamb and settled with a low growl to guard the opening.

Granny sat at the table and dropped her head in her hands.

Marshal Kent stepped beside the lady. "Ma'am, don't give up. The night is the darkest just before the dawn."

She looked up, beaming, even if tears were streaming from her eyes, "Son, I ain't giving up. I'm asking the good Lord which warpath I need to take."

The man chuckled and sat down with her to pray.

The Plan

Chapter #16

It was the dead of night when they heard a motor rumble on Main Street. A lone car stopped, and the driver's door slammed. From the sound of things, whoever had driven into Rocky Branch visited the Branch Water Brewing Company.

Ole Honker lifted his head to listen.

The two kids in the loft sat up. They had been told to go to sleep, but knowing 'Puty Sneedle was on guard outside the door kept them on edge. Besides, Granny and Marshal Kent were whispering. Plans were being made, and try as they may, Clay and Beep could not hear them.

"Thanks a lot," a man called, and before long, they heard him strolling down the alley toward the house.

All ears in the cabin were perked. The front gate creaked, waking 'Puty Sneedle from his deep sleep. He sucked in a mighty snore that sounded like a hog grubbing in the slop pit.

Beep rolled on the floor of the loft, trying to stifle giggles.

Clay choked down his laughter.

Ole Honker grumbled in his sleep. The dog dragged his eyes open, stood, stretched, and yawned.

Marshal Kent rose from his chair and quietly crossed to the door.

"Excuse me," an unknown voice spoke as he stepped up on the breezeway from outside.

All of Rocky Branch could have heard 'Puty Sneedle stumble to his feet. "Where did you come from? And how did you get into this yard? Tryin' to sneak up on me?" As an afterthought, he whipped out his gun.

"Whoa!" the man threw up his hands. "There is no need for a gun. I was told this was the Johnston place."

"So? What do you want here?" 'Puty Sneedle took a step closer.

The man kept his hands in the air. "George Washington Johnston works for me, and I am looking for him."

"You ain't going to find him, so you might as well turn yourself around and head back to the hole you crawled out from." 'Puty Sneedle sneered.

"What? And just who are you?"

"I am Deputy Sneedle. I am the law here," he thrust his head closer, "Maybe your worst nightmare."

The man took the liberty of easing the Deputy's gun aside gently. "Deputy, if you are the deputy, I found you sleeping on the breezeway, blocking the door. Highly unusual for a man of the law… unless… are you inebriated?"

"Am I what?" 'Puty Sneedle asked.

"Inebriated. Drunk." The man explained.

"No, I am not drunk. Who are you, and what are you doing here?" He rubbed his head as if it were foggy because of the deep sleep he had been awakened from.

"I need to talk with George Washington Johnston. Is this the right place? They told me at the Branch Water Brewing Company that this was it. Bedrooms and living area on one side of the house, kitchen on the other, and a breezeway in between."

"You got the right place, but you ain't going in there. I got my orders to keep everyone out, no matter who they are."

"Why?" the man wanted to know.

"That ain't none of your business."

"Deputy, I have business with this family. I have driven a long way tonight, and I see a light inside the house. I intend to knock on that door, and I intend to go inside."

"Mr., it is late, and you will have to talk to the sheriff before I let you on the inside of that door. So, you might as well be on your own sweet way." 'Puty Sneedle dropped his pistol into the holster and crossed his arms, standing firmly to bar the door.

Marshal Kent had had enough. He walked to the door, motioned Ole Honker aside, and grabbed the latch. He spoke as the door swung wide, "I am U.S. Marshal Kent, and I am inviting you in. Step aside, Deputy Sneedle."

"You can't do that," 'Puty Sneedle huffed. "I have my orders."

"And I have authority over you and your boss, Sheriff Milstrup. What I say goes. So, step aside and let this man in," Marshal Kent ordered.

"I'll go get the sheriff," 'Puty Sneedle threatened.

"You do that, 'Puty Sneedle." Marshal Kent chuckled, "You leave your post. I know your sheriff will like that. Then you tell your boss that you let someone in, and you don't know who he is. Your boss will like that, too. And when he asks you how many others came in and who all left while you were busy coming to tell him you left your post, you see how that goes." Marshal Kent chuckled and opened the door wide enough for the man to step inside.

As he started to close the door, 'Puty Sneedle stuck his foot inside the door jamb to keep it from closing. "Then I am coming in with him."

"You are not coming in, Deputy. It would be abandoning your post."

'Puty Sneedle was flustered. He wanted to come in, but he didn't want Sheriff Millstrup to be upset with him again. He didn't trust the sheriff. He stepped back and let the door close. He snuck over to the window to listen.

Granny saw him. She smiled, "Marshal, it is a bit chilly in here. Would you mind closing that window, and please go ahead and pull the curtain."

Marshal Kent laughed. He crossed to the window, winked at 'Puty Sneedle, and slammed the window down.

Granny burst into laughter, "The Lord have mercy!"

The visitor stood looking about the room, not knowing what was going on. Finally, he broke the merriment. "I am Wilber Parsons. Are you Mrs. Johnston?"

"Yes, Sir. That be me."

"Mrs. Johnston, your husband works for me."

"Mr. Parsons?" Granny looked him in the eye before she offered, "Please come to the table and have a seat."

The man took his hat off and rolled the brim until he found a peg to hang it on. Then he crossed to the table and pulled out a chair. "Thank you. Ma'am, I do not quite understand what is going on here."

Granny sighed, "I don't either, to tell you the truth, Mr. Parsons. This is U.S. Marshal Kent, and I prefer that he stay with us while we visit." She left no room for discussion.

"Of course, Mrs. Johnston," Mr. Parsons smiled. "I would welcome him."

"Then how about coffee?" she asked.

"Yes, please. It was a long drive from Farmerville, and I started after work, but I wanted to come. Actually, I felt I needed to come." He leaned back in his chair.

"That is a long drive," she said, setting the steaming cup in front of him and asking, "Cream? Sugar?"

He tried to smile, "Mrs. Johnston, I need it black. I've got to drive back tonight."

"So soon?" She nodded and sat.

Marshal Kent gave Granny an encouraging nod, refilled his own cup, and sat at the table with them.

Mr. Parsons took a good swig of his coffee before he began, "Mrs. Johnston, I could have sent a telegraph, but I wanted to come in person. Sometimes," he paused, not knowing how to explain his feelings. Boldly, he began again. "Sometimes, telegraph news gets leaked, and this is personal. Your husband has been a very dependable worker. I just promoted him to manager in charge of the pipeline here in Rocky Branch. I know times are hard with this depression, but he has not reported to work for over six shifts, and I have not been notified as to why. Ma'am, I am concerned because he was concerned about missing men and something underhanded going on. He assured me he would find out what happened to his men. That is a concern for me, since he has not shown up for work. I need to know the reason he has not reported to work." His head had dropped as he focused on the cup of coffee in front of him. "It makes no sense. He seemed so anxious to do a good job."

"No, Sir, it makes no sense," Granny said. "Thomas always does a good job, no matter what the job is."

Marshal Kent took over. He explained the things they did know. A hush settled as they told in detail about the murder of Granny's husband.

Mr. Parsons gasped, "Mrs. Johnston, I am so sorry, and that poor girl! Your granddaughter, are you positive she saw it all?"

"Yes, I did!" Beep looked over the banister, "And now 'Puty Sneedle wants to kill me because I was there. I can identify him as the murderer! I saw him kill my papa."

Clay's head popped up alongside Beep. "Sheriff Millstrup wants her dead, too. I heard him talking with 'Puty Sneedle, and they were planning to kill her."

Marshal Kent stood and paced back and forth. He sighed, "You two may as well come join us, but you must tiptoe and whisper. We cannot afford to have 'Puty Sneedle burst in."

Beep softly crawled down the ladder. Clay grabbed the ladder and stepped down two steps at a time, and halfway down, he dropped to the floor. When they were all seated at the table, Marshal Kent stopped pacing, stood, and looked around the table, "Mr. Parsons, you know what kind of man George Washington Johnston was."

"Yes, sir, I did. He was a fine man. That is why I chose him to manage the pipeline. And I know he was too good a man to be murdered like that. Lord, have mercy! Whatever is this world coming to?" He stroked the evening stubble on his chin.

Granny's eyes were glassy with unshed tears, "How am I going to protect my granddaughter? Marshal Kent, you know they will come with a search warrant first thing in the morning."

The Marshal pulled out his chair and sat back down. "Granny, do you have family or friends in another place far away from here that we could get Beep to?"

Granny set her doleful eyes on her granddaughter and talked slowly. "That is the last thing I want to do, but I know it would be the best thing for her."

"Granny, I don't want to leave you," Beep moaned. "Besides, I am the one who can hang 'Puty Sneedle. I can testify. Clay was close when 'Puty Sneedle murdered Papa, but he didn't see it happen. I was there. I saw it all."

Granny reached over and covered her granddaughter's shivering hand with hers. "Bee Poppy, Honey, I can't lose you to the likes of 'Puty Sneedle. I didn't see what he did to your papa, but you told me, and that shall be etched in my heart forever. I don't want to carry an etching of what he will do to you if he gets a chance to lay hold of you."

"But, Granny…"

"No, ma'am, I'll have no argument." She turned to Marshal Kent, "I have a sister in Dodge City, Kansas, but I have no way of getting Bee Poppy there."

The Marshal nodded. "I think I do. I have a plan." He scooted closer to the table and leaned in. When they were settled, the Marshal smiled, "The train in Farmerville."

Granny closed her eyes, "Marshal Kent, I don't have a way to get her to the train, and if I did, I don't have the money for a ticket."

"Oh," Mr. Parsons perked up and reached into his coat pocket, "I do. I brought your husband's first wages. There is plenty for a train ticket, in fact, you both could go. There is enough money for two or three tickets."

"Oh," Granny covered her heart, "Mr. Parsons, I can't leave. When they bring the pieces of my Thomas back from Monroe, I must be here to meet him." She paused, took a long breath, and said, "And I want to look into the eyes of 'Puty Sneedle and Sheriff Millstrup when they rule them guilty, and that gavel falls on the judgment." She looked down, paused for a moment, and lifted determined eyes. "And I intend to watch them hang."

"Mrs. Johnston," Wilber Parsons leaned forward, "You can't do that. Those men do not sound like men to cross."

"And I am not one to cross either, Mr. Parsons. Somehow, the truth will come out, and I would delight to see them both swing from a rope." Anger shot from her words, and she almost pounded the table with her balled fist.

Mr. Parsons sat back and shook his head. "Ma'am, I wish I could change your mind because this is dangerous business."

"You can't change my mind, Sir. Besides, I have my café to take care of, and I have always lived by this: 'I can do all things through Christ which strengtheneth me.' I have claimed that verse before, and I claim it again."

Mr. Parsons nodded, "I believe if anyone can, it would be you, Ma'am."

In his sleep, Ole Honker kicked his feet and burst forth a muffled bark. Clay thought he must agree with Granny, or he must have been dreaming of the squirrel with the crooked tail and the acorn.

Marshal Kent tapped the table. "Granny, tell me more about your sister in Kansas."

Granny grinned, "I dearly yearn to see her. Bee Poppy, she'll love you, and you'll love her. She and her husband, Martin, work at a mansion." Granny's eyes sparkled as she stood and crossed to her rugged China hutch. It was homemade and had a row of three small drawers. She pulled one open, took out a stack of letters, and carried them to the table. "I keep them all, and this is where we'll find her."

Marshal Kent took a letter and read the return address. "Kansas. Dodge City, Kansas. That is far away and ought to do the trick." He looked around the table and lowered his voice, "Wilber, are you willing to help?"

"You bet I am. I am in this all the way." His lips were in a determined line. "What do I need to do?"

The Marshal turned to the boy, "Clay, I would like for you to go on the train with Beep. I don't want Beep alone. It's too risky. And, chances are, your life is on the line, too. How about it, Clay? Would you be willing to escort this young Lady all the way to Dodge City, Kansas?"

Clay nodded. "I have never been on a train, and I want to be with Beep…so she gets there in one piece. But what about Ole Honker? Will they let him on the train?"

Marshal Kent sighed. "Under the circumstances, I think I could get him on the train, but they would want to put him in a cattle car or even cage him. I don't know how Ole Honker would feel about that. Plus, it would make your trail easier to follow: two kids and a big dog."

Clay's eyes were huge. He looked at Ole Honker, who was asleep on the floor. The dog had been to Kansas before. He was one in a litter of seven puppies born in Kansas. That's where Mama was buried. That's where Dad had knelt at the grave, laid a bundle of wildflowers, wiped his face, and grabbed Clay in a bear hug. And that's when Ole Honker yapped. Dad had smiled and teased, "Clay, is that your stomach growling?"

Clay's mouth had been a liquid smile.

Dad had gently snatched the puppy from inside his coat and dangled him in the air. "Your mom wanted you to have one of Milly's pups, and Mrs. Elma said it was fine with her."

Clay had been with Ole Honker ever since, but he knew Marshal Kent was right. Ole Honker would throw a fit being caged, and he might fight his way out of a cattle car and be lost somewhere along the train tracks forever. Clay looked at his dog with sorrow. Finally, he said, "Ole Honker is the best dog around. He could be a watch for Granny and keep her safe. He wouldn't let 'Puty Sneedle bother her. He would guard her here and at The Best Biscuits Around Café."

Granny nodded, "I would be honored, Clay, to keep Ole Honker." Then she huffed and shook her head, "I will probably have to let him inside my kitchen door."

Clay laughed, and the others joined in.

"Good. That is settled. Now, for the rest of the plan." Marshal Kent began. "We are going to make a ruckus loud enough to wake the dead, or rather 'Puty Sneedle, and we are going to play on his belief with haunts. I think haunts scare him."

Granny eyed him for a second, "Marshal, they ought to scare everyone. Haunts are of the Devil himself, and they are nothing to play with."

Marshal Kent grinned. "You are right, Granny, but I think the Lord will give his blessing this time. I think that it will keep the deputy out of our hair, and we desperately need him gone for our plan to work."

Granny sighed, "Then you have my blessing."

"Thank you." He tapped the table with his finger. "Before anything can start with the deputy, we have to get Beep and Clay out of the house."

"We could use that back window," Granny suggested.

Marshal Kent stood and walked over to the window and gazed out. All was quiet and peaceful. He tried the window, and it slid without sound. "I think that will work. Clay and Beep will sneak out this back window, and we'll close it after. I think we'll leave a crack so the two of you can hear what is going on inside. When the ruckus starts, I want you to skedaddle to Mr. Parson's car on Main Street. Hide on the floorboards. We will keep 'Puty Sneedle busy long enough to give you time to get to the car and stow away. Mr. Parsons will eventually make his way to his car and take both of you with him to the train station in Farmerville." He looked around the table. "I want your help and input on how this will play out, but first, let's pray. We need our Heavenly Father's help."

The Shiny Black Oldsmobile

Chapter #17

Stage One: Out the Window

Granny squeezed Bee Poppy tightly. She tried not to cry, but the tears would flow. "Bee Poppy, when you meet my sister, Valina, I want you to hug her for me. She'll love you the moment she lays eyes on you. Oh, how I wish I could see her, too." She took her handkerchief, edged in lace, and dabbed at her eyes. "I'll be coming to Kansas when all this hullabaloo is settled. I promise." Granny picked up a basket from the table and placed it in Beep's hand, "Here are some sandwiches for the both of you, and some of those sugar cookies you like. Don't eat them all at onest. Make them last."

Beep nodded.

Clay stood after hugging Ole Honker and giving him orders to take care of Granny. He kept his head low, slipped his sleeve across his leaking eyes, and wondered how full his gallon jar was now. He watched the floor as he shuffled toward the scene before him. He knew what it was like to leave someone you loved, especially when there was no guarantee you would ever see them again. He turned his head away. This was a private matter, and he was an outsider.

At least he was until Granny bound him in a healthy bear hug.

"Clay, you are the grandson I never had. You are a fine young man, and I know the good Lord will help you get Bee Poppy to safety. My prayers are traveling with you." She grabbed his hand and shoved a wad of bills into it. "Mr. Parsons is getting the train tickets, but this will be eating money after the sandwiches are gone, and a bit to spare for other sundry things." Then she leaned in and kissed his cheek. Clay felt his face grow hot, and he had no words to say. Finally, he choked out a "Yes, Ma'am."

Beep's face was glowing, and at any moment, laughter threatened to burst. She could tell Clay was not used to being hugged, especially by ladies.

Marshal Kent's smile stretched from one side of his face to the other. He cleared his throat, "Clay, you climb out the window first, then you can catch Beep from the other side."

Clay was glad to escape. He stepped up onto the chair and stuck his leg over the windowsill. He ducked his head through the opening and let the rest of his body follow. He dropped to the ground as quietly as he could, then he whispered, "Ready."

Beep stepped onto the chair. She turned and smiled brilliantly at her Granny. "I love you," she whispered, blew a kiss, stepped over the sill, and into Clay's arms. Gently, he placed her on solid ground.

"Remember," Mr. Parsons whispered, "my auto is the shiny black Oldsmobile. My wife makes me carry a quilt in the back seat. You can hide on the floorboard beneath it. Remember, it's the shiny black Oldsmobile."

Marshal Kent leaned against the wall by the window, "Listen, and do not run to the auto until I tell you to run for it."

Clay nodded, "Yes, Sir. We'll wait and listen." Then he heard Ole Honker whine, and Clay's heart jerked.

Marshal Kent knelt by the dog and whispered, "It will be fine, Ole Boy. I promise. It will be fine."

Stage 2: Taking Care of 'Puty Sneedle

Marshal Kent shut the window down to a crack. He wanted Beep and Clay to listen and to know what was going on inside. Then he whisked the chair away. It seemed forever, but finally, Marshal Kent pointed at Granny and whispered, "Now."

As the two outside the window watched, Granny ever so slightly smiled, then she screamed bloody murder.

Beep jumped.

"No!" Granny yelled, "No! No! It can't be! George! George! I see my George!" She fainted, dropping to the floor, and Marshal Kent swept over to catch her.

Mr. Parsons flew to the door, yanked it wide, and belted out, "Deputy! Deputy! Get in here! Quick! We need you right now."

'Puty Sneedle had been trying to listen at the door. He tumbled into the kitchen and, wildly flailing his arms, tried to keep from falling. "What's going on in here?" When he gained his balance, he threw the side of his coat back and fumbled for his gun.

Mr. Parsons stuttered, "It's…It's…the lady… Mrs. Johnston. She started pointing…pointing up there…in the loft." He pointed to the eerie black space above.

'Puty Sneedle's eyes followed Mr. Parson's finger and noticed for the first time the dark loft. He blinked, shuddered, and stared.

Mr. Parsons grabbed 'Puty Sneedle's arm and yanked him back to reality, "Then, Deputy, Mrs. Johnston muttered something that sounded like, 'George…George…George…I see George!' Then she…" Mr. Parsons swung the deputy around and leaned into his face. "I think she saw her dead husband!"

"Only his head! I only saw his head!" Granny wailed.

'Puty Sneedle sucked in a great gulp of air and shook uncontrollably.

Mr. Parsons pulled him toward the loft and spoke softly, "Then…then…she…she…yelled that his head was gone. She said it floated right off his body and out that window." He pointed to the window, and through the crack, a slight breeze fingered the curtain.

The color drained from 'Puty Sneedle's face. His eyes were wide. His Adam's apple bobbed as he gasped for air.

Marshal Kent was fanning Granny as he spoke to 'Puty Sneedle. "Deputy, go up into that loft and see if anyone is there."

"What?" 'Puty Sneedle took a step backward.

"Climb the ladder into the loft and check it out. Maybe George Washington Johnston is not dead. Maybe he is alive," Marshal Kent told him.

"Up there? I ain't going nowhere near a haunt." 'Puty Sneedle pointed to the rafters with a shaky finger. "If she saw her man, she saw a haunt 'cause he's dead! I know he is dead! You want that place checked out; you go do it your ownself. I am not. Haunts will foller you to the grave, and they will kill you when you get there." Violently, he shook his head. "No way will I set foot into that loft. I ain't going up there to find no haunt."

"Deputy, I wasn't asking. I was telling. That was an order." Marshal Kent furrowed his brow.

"It ain't an order I'm follering." His eyes were exploding with fear.

"Well then, at least look out the window. Granny said, his head floated out the window," Marshal Kent told him.

'Puty Sneedle gasped, "His head floated out a closed winder? And you want me to go see if it's there?" 'Puty Sneedle was shaking and making backward tracks toward the door.

"Deputy, if you are not going to look out that window, then I need to. Come take care of Mrs. Johnston."

"Are you off your rocker? She's the one who saw the haunt. I ain't touching her and having that haunt pass to me. Fact is, I am out of here. No way am I staying in the same room where a haunt is roaming about!" Wildly, 'Puty Sneedle turned and ran out the open door.

Silence settled over the house.

Mr. Parsons nibbled his lip and nodded, "Well, that went better than I expected. Marshal, you were right. That deputy is definitely afraid of haunts. That was a superb plan, Marshal."

Granny laughed. "I never thought it would work so well, and to my dying days, I will laugh with the memory. George would have loved to have seen that." Then Granny closed her eyes, "Dear George, my dear George." She looked back in time, sighed, and said, "Marshal, please help me up from the floor."

"Of course, Granny."

Mr. Parsons crossed to give a hand, and together, the men lifted Granny and set her in her rocker.

Granny smiled, "I don't know how much Bee Poppy and Clay got to hear, but I am sure they had enough time to sneak to Mr. Parson's auto and stow away."

Clay poked his head through the window. "We heard it all. That was the best play acting I have ever heard."

"What are you two still doing here?" Marshal Kent crossed to the window.

Clay blinked, "You told us to wait until you said, 'Run for it.' That is what you told us to do."

Marshal Kent laughed, "I guess I am the one who forgot his lines. That could have thrown a kink into everything." He turned to Granny and Mr. Parsons, "You both played your parts well, and the Lord blessed." He turned to Mr. Parsons, "I guess you can be on your way to Farmerville." He tossed his thumb toward the window, "Take those two varmints with you, and I guess you can make sure they get to the shiny black Oldsmobile. Thank you for all you have done and all you are doing."

"Yes, Mr. Parsons." Granny had her hands over her heart, "Please take care of my grandchildren, and the Good Lord, go with you."

Mr. Parsons bowed over her hand. "Yes, Ma'am. You have my sympathies for your sorrows and my prayers for blessings to come."

The Train

Chapter #18

The rocking motion of the train lulled Beep to sleep. Clay tried to close his eyes, but taking care of Beep was a big responsibility. His mind was racing faster than the train. He was in charge of getting Beep to Kansas safely. He looked out the window. He didn't know if they were still in Louisiana, but they were still in the tall, thick trees that pointed upward to heaven. The velvet of night was a cloak about them with the twinkle of stars seeping through the loosely woven threads. The chugging of the train fell into the rhythm of his heartbeat. He would miss these trees. The Kansas, he remembered, had very few trees, and the trees Kansas did have spread out like fluffy clouds on a stem sticking up in the sky instead of pointing straight to the heavens. His favorite had been an old cottonwood. He would climb up the massive trunk of the tree and spread out on a thick branch to daydream while looking through the dangling, dancing leaves. The clinking, tinkling leaves played music to his dreams. But Kansas was dry now. This was the Dirty Thirties. Rain was the prayer of even those who never prayed. Crops died of thirst, and the hope of people shriveled with the dust and was swept away by the wind. He remembered the lonely howl of the wind and the roaring attack of dust blizzards. Fingers of wind slivered through invisible cracks and choked life from all those hidden within. Clay shook his head and wondered if the dust storms still raged. Maybe they were a thing of the past?

Clay thought of his dad. Time had not given him a chance to ask Marshal Kent for news of his dad. Had Dad gotten help? Had Marshal Kent helped him? And was he still alive? Clay stuck his hand in his pocket and closed his fingers about his dad's pocket watch. He looked around. All the passengers looked like they were sleeping, and he hoped they would stay that way. Dad's pocket watch was the chain that latched him to his dad. Emotions welled up inside, and he did not wish to have an audience witness his heart on display. He held the cold metal in his fist until it warmed, then he opened his hand. Gently, he touched the spring, and the watch flipped open. He squinted to focus his eyes better. The glass was cracked, and he knew it had not been cracked before. Dad always cared for his watch because it was a special piece of family history, which he held dear. Clay looked closer and let out his breath. That was not a crack. It was a deep scratch. He rubbed his thumb over the scratch and squinted. A smile sprouted and grew. Dad had cut that scratch in the face of his watch, and Clay had no doubt about it. It was a fine arrow following the outer circumference of the watch, but it traveled counterclockwise. Clay blinked. That was important. It had to mean something. He studied the time the watch held: six fifteen. He looked out the train window. It was already daylight, and that meant it was past six fifteen. He held the watch to his ear and heard nothing. Maybe it had stopped. He studied the watch. It had stopped, alright. The little knob that set the hands on the watch was gone. There was no way he could move the watch hands to make it report the correct time. Had his dad stopped his watch on these numbers for a purpose? He narrowed his eyes and thought on the matter. Finally, he nodded. If his dad cut an arrow on the face of his pocket watch, Clay knew he had set the hands in the place he wanted them to stay. Then he must have pulled the knob off the watch to guarantee the hands pointed to the numbers he had set. It had to be a clue. But a clue to what? Dad must be trying to tell him something.

"Lord," he whispered, "I need your help. Dad wants me to read his clues, and I am having trouble."

Beep squirmed and stretched.

Clay tucked the watch back into his pocket.

The girl's eyes cracked a slit and then slid closed again. She moaned and dropped her head to Clay's shoulder.

Clay sucked in his breath. Now, he couldn't move. He didn't want to wake her. He shut his eyes, but he couldn't sleep. Dad wasn't with him, and Ole Honker was left behind. He held a message close in his pocket, but he didn't know what it meant. The message was from Dad, so with the Lord's help, he should be able to figure it out. He had been with Dad all his life. If anyone could figure out the message, it should be him.

"Papa, Papa, no…" Beep whimpered.

Clay's heart beat a little faster. If Beep was dreaming about her papa, it was not a restful dream. Clay waited, and Beep settled soundly to sleep.

Clay's thoughts raced back to his dad's watch. Dad had asked Mr. Kent to make sure he gave the watch to his son. Clay narrowed his eyes. Had Dad told Mr. Kent what the watch meant? Moments passed. Clay decided Mr. Kent did not know, or he would have been asking questions. At least Clay didn't have to decide whether to tell Mr. Kent because Mr. Kent was not with them to tell. "Good," he whispered.

Clay leaned back in his seat. Trees zipped by the window, but they were changing. No longer were the trees pointing tall and straight to the sky, but now they were fat, bushy, and full of color. Still, they were lush and begged for a picnic beneath their branches.

Serenaded by the chugging engine and grinding wheels, Clay nestled down and gave way to sleep. His last thoughts were of Dad, wounded, sick, lying in a damp, dark cave. But…why? He drifted into the thick sleep of exhaustion. The world of dreams took over his being.

Dreaming…Each step he took echoed. It was dark, and he had to run his hand along the rock wall to know where to place his foot for his next step. The wall was rough, cold, and damp. Shivers raced up his spine. "Hello?" he called.

"Hello… hello… hello…each echo dwindled into a hush, but he had to keep going. Dad was hidden in some dark recess of this cave… and Dad needed him. His life depended on Clay finding him in time. Clay wanted to call out to his dad, but what if he wasn't alone? A shiver seized his body, and the lantern shook in his hand, awakening shadows that danced across the walls. He kicked a stone and listened to it cascade deep below. He gasped and plastered himself against the rock wall. His heart pounded. The stone splashed. At least Dad had water… if he could get to it. Clay tried to remember what Arthur Kent had said. Had he even mentioned water in the cave? The boy calmed his breathing and took another step. He slipped and wildly tried to grab anything. He gasped as bats swarmed his head. A big bat swooped in his face, but the bat had no head! "Yeow!" he yelled.

Hands grabbed him and shook his body.

With arms flailing, Clay fought what he thought was the beheaded bat. "No! No!"

"Clay! Wake-up! You are scaring the bejeebies out of me!" Beep was in his face, and her eyes held terror.

Clay was shaking, but he managed to mumble, "Sorry. I am so sorry. I think I was fighting the bejeebies myself."

"I think you were dreaming. You want to tell me about it?" Beep asked.

"No! That wasn't a dream. That was a nightmare! And I may never want to talk about it." He swallowed and tried to slow his heart. He couldn't tell Beep about the headless bat. It would remind her of her papa. He tried to close his eyes, but when he did, he saw thousands of bats swarming.

"Clay? Do you want one of Granny's sandwiches?" Beep whispered.

"Sandwich?" Now, his stomach calmed. Perfect. One of Granny's sandwiches would fit the bill. "You bet I do."

Beep giggled, "Granny always said the way to a man's heart was through his stomach." She pulled one from the hamper and handed it to Clay.

The boy closed his eyes and prayed. "Dear Jesus, thank you for this sandwich and Granny who made it. Please help me forget that nightmare and never have it again! Amen." He bit a hunk of sandwich and chewed.

Beep looked at him. "You really believe God hears your prayers?"

Clay waited to answer Beep until he swallowed. "I do."

"Really?" Beep crossed her arms. "My papa is dead, and I prayed God would protect us. Your dad is gone and has been for days, over a week and a half, and maybe longer. What makes you think there is a God who hears your prayers and answers them?"

That was a question Clay wished his dad could have answered. He took another bite of the sandwich to give him time to think. He chewed. He swallowed. "Beep, I have Jesus in my heart. I have been talking to him for a long time, so I know He answers my prayers in the best way for me. Sometimes the answer comes as a 'yes,' and," he sighed, "sometimes it comes as a 'no.' Sometimes, He wants us to wait until He is ready to answer."

"Granny has told me that before." Her eyes did not look convinced as she stared at Clay.

Clay took another bite and chewed with thought. He waved his sandwich at the girl next to him, "Beep, is that the only thing you asked God that night?"

She squinted her eyes, "What do you mean?"

"I mean, did you ask God to help Granny not catch you when you snuck out to follow your papa that night?"

Beep pressed her lips together, "That is none of your business."

Clay laughed. "You did, didn't you?"

"So." She glared. "If Granny had caught me, you know, she wouldn't have let me go. I needed to be with Papa, so, yes. I asked God to keep Granny from catching me."

He held up a finger, "Answer to prayer number one. God said, 'Yes.'"

Beep drew in a deep breath.

"Then," Clay continued, "I'll bet you asked God to help you find your papa and to help your papa say you could stay with him and not send you back home."

The girl crossed her arms and refused to answer.

The boy laughed again, but he didn't let it go. "That was the answer to your prayer number two. "God said, 'Yes.'"

Beep pressed her lips together.

"Then when 'Puty Sneedle had you cornered, I'll bet you asked God to help you get away."

Beep sealed her lips as a light was beginning to shine in her eyes.

"Answer to prayer number three, 'Yes.'" Clay gloated. "Then, I bet you prayed that I was a safe guy when I found you."

When Beep didn't answer, Clay chuckled. "Answer to prayer number four, 'Yes.'"

Beep stared at the seat in front of her.

"Did you pray that I would get you safe home to your granny's?"

Beep's lips trembled.

"Prayer number five? God answered, 'Yes.'"

Tears were rolling down Beep's cheeks. "But God didn't answer the most important prayer I ever had. My papa is dead."

"Beep," Clay whispered, "Maybe that wasn't your papa's prayer. Maybe he prayed God would keep you safe at all costs. Maybe he was the cost of your safety."

"Oh," she groaned. She leaned back and closed her eyes tight.

"That fight between your papa, even though he was already in the arms of Jesus, and 'Puty Sneedle gave you time to escape." Clay paused. "I don't understand all the ways of God; I just trust Him to care for me."

Sobs were shaking the girl's body. "But I did not want that answer! I wanted my papa. So, why did God take him? Why?"

The word hung in the air like thick moss from a sweet gum tree. Clay didn't have an answer, but his heart was as broken as hers. Her head fell on his shoulder, and Clay held his breath as she nestled against him. He closed his eyes and felt tears prying from them. The harder he tried not to cry, the closer the dam holding his tears came to breaking. Oh, that jar of tears in heaven must be a five-gallon pickle jug by now.

Kansas

Chapter #19

For two days, they rode the Kansas City Southern Railway across Louisiana, Arkansas, and Missouri. In Kansas City, they had to change rail lines. The Kansas City station was huge and busy, but they had a few hours to catch the Atchison, Topeka, and Santa Fe heading for Dodge City.

The whistle blew, and the train screamed to a stop. People stood, stretched, and latched onto their bags. Then, like a flood, people rushed toward the door. Clay kept close to Beep.

On the landing, Clay took a deep breath. It wasn't the clear, clean air he was used to. This air was thick with city smells. The platform was made of 2x12s, smoothly worn boards. It was almost impossible to step quietly, but they would leave no sign on those smooth boards. Like it or not, they became part of the crowd. The only place to go was inside the station.

Once in the crowd, Clay decided he did not like cities. No matter where he turned, someone was always there. He didn't like people brushing against him and bumping into him. He didn't like the noise the crowd made. Dad had taught him to listen to sounds because they were clues to survival. He could feel panic rising. What if he lost Beep? She could get cut off in the crowd and be out of sight instantly. She was his responsibility. Did he dare grab her hand? What if it startled her and she doubled her fist and decked him? What if she screamed? What would the crowd do? He knew. They would attack him, because any guy who would touch a young woman was in the wrong. Everyone would come to her rescue. Clay was sweating. He swiped his forehead with his forearm and looked over the crowd.

His heart lurched to a stop. Across the wave of heads, he saw a man who reminded him of 'Puty Sneedle. Could there be another? For a moment, he couldn't breathe. No. There was no other. There was only one 'Puty Sneedle in this world, and that had to be him. He grabbed Beep's arm and yanked her around a corner and through a doorway.

"What was that for?" she stomped her foot, wiggled away from Clay, and glared.

Clay hum-hawed, searching for an answer because he didn't want to frighten Beep. It scared him that someone even looked like 'Puty Sneedle, and the chances were that no one did. That meant it had to be 'Puty Sneedle. But how? They had left Rocky Branch in the dead of night, hidden beneath blankets in the Oldsmobile. Again, he wiped the sweat from his brow.

Before him, Beep was tapping her foot, waiting for an answer.

A lady in a green felt hat with yellow flowers rounded the corner. She stopped, threw her hands in the air, flipping her yellow purse madly about her head, and gasped, "Young man, just what are you doing in the ladies' parlor? I ought to call the police. You can be arrested for coming in here." She blinked, "In fact, that is exactly what I am going to do. I just passed a nice policeman out in the lobby." She pointed her finger at Clay. "He will take care of the likes of you! Intruding in the Ladies' Parlor!" She swung about to march out the door.

Clay's eyes bulged in terror, "Please, Ma'am, I didn't know what room this was. It was an accident. I didn't know it was the Ladies' Parlor! I am leaving." He stutter-stepped wide around the woman and ran.

The lady smashed herself against the wall, getting out of his way. "Well, I never… and I guess I won't need that policeman now. Too bad, he was a nice-looking young policeman," she said with regret, straightened her hat, and slid the handle of her purse back over her shoulder.

When the lady had gone about her business, Beep flew out of the ladies' parlor, caught up with Clay, and doubled over in laughter. Finally, she caught her breath and warned Clay, "You had better watch what you are doing. The police will be on your trail."

Clay shoved his hands in his pockets, but he still didn't mention 'Puty Sneedle. He had missed the man altogether when he was hoping for a good look from behind the wall of that room. He had a gut feeling the man had to be 'Puty Sneedle. He had best keep his eyes open.

Finally, they boarded their train. Clay was relieved. 'Puty Sneedle or any man looking like him had not followed them aboard. He sat back to watch out the window as the train rumbled across the Kansas lands. The further west they traveled, the more the country changed. The land was parched. The grass was brown, and the air smelled of dust. It looked just like Clay remembered, and it sounded the same. A lonely howl in the wind seemed to leak through the train windows and sink into his soul.

Beep squinted out the window. "There's not much to see in Kansas, is there?"

Clay shook his head.

"I'll bet you don't eat many fish out here. We haven't crossed a bridge in miles. And the last river we saw didn't have enough water for minnows to swim in." Beep sighed.

Clay smiled. Kansas did not appeal to many people. There were mostly farmers and ranchers, when there was rain, but it held a special place in his heart. Until one lays their eyes on a God-painted sunrise or sunset over the Kansas prairies, one could not know the beauty of the land.

"What do you do here, anyway?" she complained.

Clay shrugged. So many people thought there was nothing to the prairies of Kansas, and he loved the land. Inside, he grinned before he answered Beep. "Hunt buffalo."

She whipped her head around. "You have hunted buffalo?"

He shrugged, "There are not many left, and with this drought, they have gone to greener pastures. There are no green pastures in Kansas."

Beep narrowed her eyes. "Then why did you say you hunted buffalo?"

His smile touched a flare to his eyes. "Because I wanted to hunt buffalo instead of rabbits."

The girl shook her head. "Why?"

"It would have been exciting, and we could have fed a whole lot of people. It would have helped." Clay looked beyond her and out the window. He didn't want to talk. He had only mentioned the buffalo because once, his dad had made a comment about how much more meat would be on a buffalo than on a rabbit. And, honestly, he had wished to shoot a buffalo.

Beep wrinkled her nose, "Skinning a buffalo would have been a lot of work."

Clay laughed. "It would have been a lot of meat, too."

Beep leaned back. "This land is tiring. It's just grass, grass, and more grass, and it's all brown."

Clay's eyes twinkled, "And your Louisiana is just trees, trees, and more trees, and they all have moss hanging from them."

Beep laughed. It was laughter that washed away her complaint, and Clay liked it.

Beep settled back and closed her eyes.

He studied the land flying by the window. This was the land that had claimed his mom, and memories like a downpour of badly needed rain flooded his thoughts. A faint smile touched his lips. His thoughts were flooded in the midst of a dry, cracked land. His heart felt that way: dry and cracked and yet somehow drowning.

He licked his chapped lips and closed his eyes. He had left Mom in the Kansas dirt and Dad in a damp, wet cave somewhere in Louisiana. It didn't matter if it was wet or dry. They were still gone. "Dear Lord," he whispered, "I feel so alone. I need your help."

The moment he prayed, he felt Beep turn away from him. He peeked and sighed. She was watching out the window. His next prayer made no sound. It was between God and himself. "Dear Jesus, please reach into Beep's heart and help her believe you answer prayers in your time, in your way, and for our good."

The train rattled across the parched prairie land, and Beep gave way to sleep.

The boy looked at the Kansas sky. Kansas sunsets were extraordinary, and he had missed them. The whole sky seemed to be God's palette. Pastel colors streamed and flowed, whisking across the horizon and leaving ribbon trails for the imagination to tag, hold, and follow. Somehow, this whole sky covered all of America and more. The engine's smoke sent up a charcoal film, dooming the brilliant sunset to the coming dark night.

With hope, he prayed Beep had witnessed the sunset. Clay looked at the girl next to him. Her eyes were closed, and her lips drooped.

Clay settled back into his seat. Maybe another time, the Kansas sunset would catch her heart. He shoved his hand into his pocket. His dad's watch. He felt the cold metal grow warm in his hand. He knew the etching on the watch's face was a clue from his dad. It meant something. But what? He sighed and pulled out his dad's watch. He stared at it. That arrow had to be a clue. He blinked, trying to get the cobwebs out of his head. He had to remember Dad and how Dad thought. He looked over at Beep and smiled. That girl was sawing some big logs, and she might be sawing for a long time. With everything that had happened, she had to be worn out. He was.

He gazed over the other passengers. Most were settling since the sun had dropped from the sky. The porter was making his way down the aisle, lighting the lamps at the front and back of the train car.

Clay nestled back and closed his eyes. He intended to pretend to sleep, and when all was quiet, he planned to study his dad's pocket watch and figure out what the clues meant.

The iron wheels whirred over the rails, and the train car rocked. Clay took a deep breath and sighed. Sleep slipped her long fingers through his hair and gently caressed his temples. He relaxed, sagged against the back of his seat, and gave way to sleep.

A Shot in the Night

Two cars back, "Puty Sneedle blew hot breath on his badge to steam clean it. With the point of his pocketknife, he flaked off rust where the dried blood had been. Then he spit on his badge, took his handkerchief, and polished the metal. With a sigh of satisfaction, 'Puty Sneedle slipped his badge into his shirt pocket and patted it as if tucking it into bed. No one was going to call him 'Puty Sneedle anymore. He had high-tailed it out of that God-forsaken Louisiana timberland and headed west. Those kids had slipped out of his fingers one too many times, and he knew Sheriff Millstrup. He had no give in him at all. Sheriff Millstrup had as much as said that if he lost those kids again, he, Deputy Irwin Sneedle, was a dead man. Well. He had lost them again. But... even Sheriff Millstrup could not kill or have killed what he could not find. 'Puty Sneedle was headed for the mountains of Colorado and a cabin he had found high up in those mountain peaks. He narrowed his eyes and raked through all the memories in his mind. Had he ever mentioned Colorado and that peaceful cabin to Sheriff Millstrup? He shook his head. "No." He was sure that was his secret. 'Puty Sneedle wedged into the back of his seat, stretched out his long, bony legs, closed his eyes, and welcomed sleep. He intended to dream of the Colorado Rockies.

A Shot in the Night

Dodge City

Chapter #20

The train whistle cut through the early morning, and Clay jumped. He sucked in a bunch of air, causing a loud gurgling sound to erupt from his throat, followed by a coughing volcano.

Wide-eyed, Beep smashed back against the window and braced herself. "Hey, Clay, are you going to be all right?"

Clay looked around and grinned. "Guess I was dreaming."

"Well, next time, dream a little quieter, and with your mouth closed. You almost scared me to death, and I think you woke up the back half of the train car." Beep giggled.

Clay shrugged, glancing behind and catching the smiles of fellow passengers. He grinned, "I didn't mean to. That train whistle blew while I was dreaming." He leaned closer to Beep. "We were on the river, and an alligator, a monster alligator with yellow glow-in-the-dark eyes, had just snapped my oar in half. His teeth had wet moss sliming from them." Clay spread his fingers and dragged his hands down from his mouth over the front of his shirt, following imaginary strings of moss. He leaned in close and grinned, "Then, that monster alligator flipped his tail and almost rocked the boat over and dumped us into the deep, murky water thick with gators!"

Beep cringed. "Back up. I don't need to hear any more of your dreams. They are all too real. Keep them to yourself."

The train whistle blew again, and they could feel the brakes grinding against the wheels skidding on the tracks.

Everyone was awake now.

The porter stepped into their car and pulled the door shut behind him, smothering the outside noise with a cloud of smoke. "Next stop, Dodge City, Kansas."

Clay smoothed down his jacket over his shirt and caught his breath. Quickly, he slipped his hand into his pocket. He gasped. No watch. His heart pounded faster. He had had the watch in his hand last night when he had pretended to go to sleep. He swallowed. That was his dad's watch, and that watch was his only clue to something important his dad wanted to tell him. Now it was gone. Clay stood. Maybe it was in his seat. But his seat was empty. He had to have that watch. He dropped to the floorboards searching beneath his seat. Nothing. He could not get off the train in Dodge City, and he couldn't let Beep get off the train in Dodge City without him. He could not step off this train without his Dad's watch. He jumped to his feet and began searching all his pockets. Nothing. Then he noticed the glint in Beep's eyes. Right in front of him, she dangled his treasure.

"Looking for this?" she smiled. "It fell out of your hand sometime in the night and caught on my skirt."

Clay grabbed the watch. "Thank you. Oh. Beep, thank you. It was my dad's watch, and I thought I had lost it."

"I understand." Beep's eyes softened as she reached into her bag, pulled out her papa's Scottish cap, and gently placed it on her head.

The smile they shared shut out the whole world.

"Young man," the porter called, "You had best be seated when we pull into the station and stop. You might fly over the seat in front of you, and that passenger would not like you in her lap. Need I say the persons behind you would not thank you either if they happened to be the lucky target." The porter chuckled as the boy scrambled into his seat.

Beep plastered her hat tightly on her head and held onto her bag.

The train wheels rang, and the pressure of the stop pushed them both into the backs of their seats.

Smoke rolled over the top of the train cars and settled to cover the platform like fog over the river. The whistle blew, the train jerked to a stop, and everyone stood to push their way to the door.

Beep and Clay held back. Clay could see the fear in her eyes. They were to meet her Aunt Valina, who was a sister to her Granny. Clay wondered if they looked alike, and what if they acted alike? Maybe they would have a sign made and held high reading, “Bee Poppy.” He had seen those welcome signs in the stations along the way.

When they stepped out onto the platform, the crowd began to clear away. Clay scanned the station. Mr. Kent had said he would get a telegraph message to Beep’s Aunt, so she should be here. Clay surveyed the crowd, searching for someone who resembled Granny or someone holding a welcome sign.

Beep grabbed his arm and gasped.

She must have found her Aunt Valina.

The smoke lifted, and across the platform slouched ‘Puty Sneedle.

Clay’s heart lurched as much as the train had done.

“Hey!” ‘Puty Sneedle narrowed his eyes as they settled on the two, and he yelled, “I gotcha now!” He sprang and lunged in their direction.

Clay didn’t bother to tell Beep to run. He yanked her arm, and they flew off the side of the platform. With a stumble, he caught Beep and steadied her on her feet. His heart beat a bit faster. He shivered, then he grabbed her arm and ran. Smoke was still settling, and for a moment, they were erased from sight. Clay stopped and ducked beneath the platform, pulling Beep with him. He crawled deeper into the dark shadow, and he plastered his finger against his lips to convey silence. His heart was pounding so loudly that he was glad for the trampling of feet overhead.

He looked at the girl crouching beside him. Tear after silent tear rolled. "How did he follow us? How did he find out where we were going?"

"I don't know, Beep. I don't know," Clay spoke low.

"I hope Granny is alright." The girl shook.

"Lord Jesus, hide us from 'Puty Sneedle like you hide our sins as far away as the east is from the west," he whispered. "And please let Granny be fine."

Beep studied him. "I hope your Lord Jesus will answer your prayers."

"He will, but Beep," he pleaded, "you can make it your prayer, too."

She closed her eyes without a word, and Clay wondered if she was hugging a prayer or hiding from one.

That was when Clay saw 'Puty Sneedle's legs. He would know those boots anywhere, and the man seemed to be standing. Waiting. Watching. Searching.

Clay wanted to let Beep know, but what if she said something? What if she jumped and hit the platform?

The girl shivered and looked into his eyes, "How close is 'Puty Sneedle?"

"Just his legs right over there," He pointed. "Don't make a sound," he mouthed the words.

People were crossing the platform, but Clay could tell they were dwindling in number. The boy licked his lips and tasted the dust settling from above. Soon it would be only 'Puty Sneedle, Beep, and himself.

Beep didn't move, and Clay listened to hear her breath.

She was so quiet that he wrapped his arm about her. He could feel her heart pounding.

'Puty Sneedle slapped his hand on the top of the platform and belted out a few choice words, followed by, "I know I saw those slippery, stinking kids. It had to be them. But what would they be doing here? Oh…" he slammed a fist against the thick boards above the 'stinking kids' and whistled. "They must have followed me! I hope they did. I'll show them!" He stomped away in the dust.

Clay swallowed, "Let's stay here for a little bit. I don't want our paths to cross 'Puty Sneedle again, not in this lifetime."

Beep nodded. "I'm with you on that. I don't want to see him again, but…" She shuddered as her eyes wandered about, "This place gives me the creeps. It must be a spider's mansion."

Clay looked at her. She was right. A spider's web clung to her Papa's cap, but Clay was not going to tell her.

It was quiet, and 'Puty Sneedle had long ago disappeared, Clay moved. "I think it should be safe enough now, and let's pray he gets on another train and leaves the country."

Beep nodded, but she did not commit to pray.

Even if it was safe, Clay made sure they crawled out the other side of the platform.

No one was waiting for Beep. No one looked like her granny, and no one held a welcome sign. The train yard was almost empty. The restaurant across the way held people from their train, and that meant it might also have 'Puty Sneedle. Quickly, he took Beep's arm and pulled her into the shadows on the other side of the station.

Beep dusted off her skirts and dropped onto an old bench. "Now, what do we do?"

Clay took off his hat and rolled the brim in his hands. He stared at the web on Beep's cap. He wanted to laugh, but the girl across from him might not take that well. Slowly, he reached over and took Beep's cap and whopped it against his leg. As he handed it back, his eyes sparkled, "I think you were right. There must be a herd of spiders living under there."

The girl shivered, jumped up, danced wildly in a circle, and shook her skirts, but she did not yell.

Clay tried to swallow his laughter, but it burst out.

Beep glared. She put her hands on her hips and stomped. "I hope there are bunches of spiders down the back of your shirt!"

Clay laughed louder, but suddenly he could feel them crawling on his back. He yanked the shirt off and whacked it desperately on the platform.

Beep doubled over. When she could catch her breath, she shoved out the words, "By now? Those spiders are either all gone or flattened dead!"

"Dead, I hope." Clay grinned.

Together, they collapsed on the bench as their laughter settled into a chuckle and then a twinkling smile.

"Now what do we do?" Beep asked.

Clay twisted his lips in thought. "I think we'll find the sheriff's office. He could help us locate your Aunt Valina.

She smiled at him. "That is a good idea, Clay."

For some reason, the boy's cheeks warmed. He dipped his head and looked away from the girl.

The Sheriff's office was not hard to find. It was built right in the middle of Main Street, Dodge City, Kansas. A big sign hung above the door, which read, "Sheriff's Office, Sheriff Paul Ary Residing."

Clay looked up and down the street before he went to the door. Just as he grabbed the doorknob, he heard voices inside.

"I tell you, Sheriff Ary, I saw them get off the train right here in your town, Dodge City, Kansas."

Clay recognized that voice. He backed away from the door, pulling Beep with him, and stood to listen through the open window of the sheriff's office. 'Puty Sneedle's back was toward Clay and Beep. Sheriff Ary had his eyes fixed on the man standing in front of his desk.

Clay put his finger to his lips, and together they listened.

The Sheriff held up his hand, "Whoa. Slow down, Mister, and let's start over. And, let's start with your name."

'Puty Sneedle took a deep breath. "Deputy Irwin Sneedle from Rocky Branch, Louisiana, and I tell you, those two kids are runaways."

"Runaways?" The sheriff leaned forward and tapped his desk with his forefinger. "Runaways? I haven't seen any posters or warrants for runaways come across my desk. Do you have papers on them? I'd like to see them."

"Papers? Of course, there are papers." He started patting his pockets. I've got them somewhere," he lied.

Beep whispered, "Do you think there are papers on us?"

Clay shook his head. "'Puty Sneedle is lying. I can tell. He wouldn't look straight on at the sheriff, and he has that nervous thing where he starts stoking the butt of his gun."

Beep's eyes dropped to 'Puty Sneedle's hand dangling close to his holster. Sure enough, he was rubbing the gun butt.

'Puty Sneedle pressed his lips together, "Them papers must be in my saddle bags."

"Well, pull up a chair and dig. You dropped your saddle bags on the floor when you busted in here."

'Puty Sneedle's eyebrows jumped high as he dropped his gaze to his beat-up saddle bags on the floor at his boots. Slowly, he stepped to a chair, grabbed the back of it, swung it around, and set it in front of the sheriff's desk. He talked as he reached for his saddlebags. "I been after those two more than a week now. They are slippery as a greased hog." He paused and pointed his finger at the sheriff, "And they are mean, downright devil mean."

Sheriff Ary drew his eyebrows together. "Just how old are we talking about?"

"I'd say they just stepped into what people been callin' the teen years."

"Twelve? Thirteen?"

"Yep, but, Sheriff, they are mean…real mean."

"At twelve or thirteen? Just how can they be that mean?" Sheriff Ary pressed his eyes into those of 'Puty Sneedle.

"Puty Sneedle stood, put his hands on the edge of the sheriff's desk, and leaned in, "Sheriff, I met that girl…"

"A girl? One is a girl?" Sheriff Ary asked.

"You better bet your boots she's a girl, and a right down mean girl. I met her in the moonlight along the Quachita River, and that girl killed her own grandpa. I saw the whole thing."

Sheriff Ary squinted at the man before him, "She is 11 or 12 years old?"

"She don't care she's eleven or twelve. She aimed that gun and blew him away! Her own grandpa!"

"You stood there and watched her shoot him? You didn't try to stop her?"

"I saved my hide, Sheriff." He poked his own chest with his forefinger as he talked. "What good would I be dead? At least I can tell people what happened."

Outside, Beep's mouth dropped open, and fire shot from her eyes. She threw her papa's cap on the boardwalk and started toward the door.

Clay grabbed her arm and swung her around. "You can't march in there like that. 'Puty Sneedle might shoot you, but he would for sure have you."

The girl hesitated for a minute.

'Puty Sneedle didn't. "When we went back and found the body, we only found the head hanging from a tree branch. It looked to have been chopped off the body, and she must have rolled the body into the river for the gators to destroy all evidence."

"Why?"

'Puty Sneedle shrugged. "Maybe Voodoo, maybe a warning 'cause she's a witch woman. We got a plenty of them witch women in the bayou."

"But you said she was eleven or twelve."

"They start them witch women young," 'Puty Sneedle shivered. His lie had made his skin crawl.

Witch Girl

Chapter #21

Beep had had enough. She stomped her foot, marched to the door, and yanked it open. She pointed her finger and accused, "That man, 'Puty Sneedle, is a liar! I did not kill my papa. He killed my papa. I watched him shoot him in cold blood! He shot him dead! Then he tried to kill me."

'Puty Sneedle whipped about to face the girl. His heart skipped a beat as he was drawn into her raging eyes. Anger like hot lava was boiling and ready to spew from a volcano. Any second now, that girl was going to erupt.

'Puty Sneedle backed against the wall, his eyes smoking with fear.

Beep stomped across to stand in front of him. She poked him in the stomach to accent each word she spoke. "I saw you shoot my papa in cold blood, and I watched you fight with his dead body and scream like a banshee when you thought he had a death grip on you and was pulling you down to Hell where you belong!"

'Puty Sneedle couldn't talk. For a few long seconds, he couldn't breathe. His eyes seemed to be glued to the witch girl's eyes, and he could not pull them away. He was smashed against the back wall of the sheriff's office, and he didn't think there was a back door. He had made up the story of this girl being involved in Voodoo and being a witch woman, but what if she really was? His hands were trembling, and his heart was racing. Could she kill him with her Voodoo? He had to close his eyes before that witch girl looked deep into them and captured his soul! And, try as he might, he could not close them! He had no power over his own eyes! 'Puty Sneedle whined in hopelessness.

Wide-eyed, Sheriff Ary leaned back in his chair and watched the scene unfold. From the first, he hadn't fully trusted Deputy Sneedle. This encounter shed a bit of shady light on the man.

Clay was frozen. They had made it all the way to Dodge City, Kansas, safely, but he sure could not protect Beep now. He looked around. He was standing in the sheriff's office, and he couldn't even remember stepping through the door.

'Puty Sneedle screamed like a girl and sank to the floor, holding his eyes so the girl could not look into them.

Beep leaned in closer, "I saw what you did to my papa. But you need to know that God watched it all. God is Almighty, and God takes care of his own. My papa belonged to God, so you had better watch every step you take because God will collect."

Chills like a million army ants march up 'Puty Sneedle's back. He screamed, jumped from the floor, and started to run.

Clay blocked his way.

'Puty Sneedle's vision was blurry, and he crashed into the boy and screeched, "No! No, you devil! You can't have me! You can't drag me to Hell! I'm not ready to die!" He turned and ran the only way left to run. He threw himself into an empty cell and slammed the door shut. He scrambled to the cot and rolled into a ball, sobbing.

The eerie sobbing cloaked the room with dark foreboding.

Sheriff Ary stood and swallowed. "Now, I've never had that happen before. He shut his own self in the cell." He shook his head, pulled the keys from his desk drawer, walked to the cell, and locked it.

Beep shook as if waking from a trance.

Clay was cold and sweating at the same time.

In the silence that followed, Sheriff Ary turned to the two kids. "So, are you two runaways, as he said?" He tossed his thumb across his shoulder toward the cell and 'Puty Sneedle.

Beep stepped close to Clay and shook her head.

Clay spoke, "No, Sir. We were sent here. Beep has an aunt we were supposed to meet when we got off the train, but we didn't see her. We saw 'Puty Sneedle instead."

Beep shivered. "And he saw us."

Clay nodded. "We ran and hid under the platform at the train station until 'Puty Sneedle left. We didn't think he would come here in a million years. We came because we thought you might help us." Clay explained.

Sheriff Ary studied them. "What do you know about the deputy over there?" He nodded toward the cell.

Beep stepped in with her fists balled. "He lies. He steals. He kills people, and he cuts up their bodies."

Sheriff Ary drummed his fingers on his desk as he studied the girl. He turned his eyes on Clay. "Young man, what do you know of the deputy?"

"I didn't see him kill Beep's papa, but I heard the shot. I did see him fighting with her papa's dead body. It looked like her papa was alive from the dead, and I think God was in that. It allowed Beep to get away from 'Puty Sneedle before he could kill her. And, believe me, 'Puty Sneedle was going to kill her, and he has been trying to kill her ever since."

Sheriff Ary pressed his lips together in a grim line.

Beep stepped in, "That's when I ran into Clay, and he wouldn't let me go back to my papa. He made me get in his boat with him and Ole Honker."

"Ole Honker?" the sheriff asked.

"My hunting dog, Sir," Clay answered. "He's a good ole dog, and he took to Beep right away. I guess he knew she needed him."

"And where did all of this happen?"

"Rocky Branch, Louisiana, Sir, or thereabouts," Clay said.

"When I telegraph the sheriff in Rocky Branch, what will I hear from him?"

Clay pulled in a ragged breath. "Sheriff Millstrup? It won't be good. He and 'Puty Sneedle are partners."

Sheriff Ary nodded and placed his elbows on his desk. He dropped his chin and cradled it in his hands while he thought.

Finally, he turned to the girl and asked, "Who is your aunt?"

Wildly, Beep's eyes shifted, "Valina, Sir. Right now, I can't remember her last name, but my granny said she works at a mansion.

The sheriff smiled. "Well, I might know who she is." He stood and stretched in thought. Finally, he turned with decision and swept the jail keys from the top of his desk. "I have a few things I need to check on, and I want you here when I come back. I don't think you are runaways, but I want to be sure you are here when I get back. Both of you step into the other jail cell.

Clay swallowed, "You are going to lock us in jail?"

"Only until I am sure of who you are and where you go." The sheriff herded them into the jail cell and shut the door. The key made no noise in the well-oiled lock, and Sheriff Ary winked as he turned to go. "It's only until I find out what to do with you Younguns."

"But we are right next to 'Puty Sneedle!" Beep protested.

Sheriff Ary raised his eyebrows, "He can't get to you, I guarantee it, and both of you seem smart enough to stay out of his reach. Besides. He looks like he is going to hibernate."

"But we'll be alone with HIM!" Beep complained.

Sheriff Ary grinned, "My deputy will check in. That ought to keep things in order, and I won't be gone long."

Beep crossed her arms and glowered.

Sheriff Ary winked.

Beep looked at Clay and at the cot. She grabbed the closest leg of the cot and dragged it as far away from 'Puty Sneedle's cell as she could get. Then she plopped down and crossed her arms. She refused to look at Sheriff Ary as tears welled up in her eyes. Why? She had escaped 'Puty Sneedle only to be caged miles away from home in the cell right next to his. She glared at Clay. "You go ahead and pray to your God, but I don't think he is listening."

Clay shrugged and grinned. "Beep. 'Puty Sneedle is locked up. He can't get to us."

"So," she wailed, "We are locked up, too, and we are right beside him." She gritted her teeth. "I can smell him!"

Clay laughed, "You can't smell him, Beep."

She grinned wickedly, "Then it must be you I smell."

Clay's eyebrows shot up. "Oh?" he headed toward her.

Sheriff Ary chuckled. "I have several sets of handcuffs. If I need to, I can cuff both of you to the loops in the walls so you can't reach each other. Do I need to do that so you will both be safe until I return?"

Beep glared.

Clay laughed, "No, Sir. We will be fine."

"Good. I'll bring some vittles when I come back." He took his hat from the peg beside the door and slapped it on his head.

Clay's tummy growled. Usually, he would blame it on Ole Honker, but Ole Honker wasn't here. He was at home keeping Granny safe.

Beep narrowed her eyes. Then she spread her hands wide, and in an eerie voice she crooned, "Come sit with me."

Clay looked twice before he chuckled, "Witch Girl?"

The Pocket Watch

Chapter #22

Beep studied the ceiling, and Clay knew she was not in a talking mood. He left her alone, even though he sat beside her on the cot. Across the cell, 'Puty Sneedle slept.

Clay slipped his hand into his pocket and pulled out his dad's watch. He rubbed the gold lid with his thumb, opening memories of his dad, rushing through time and settling in his beating heart. Dad. Was he still hanging on to life, or had he stepped into eternity? Clay's shoulders sagged. Would he ever know? For a moment, he pulled his dad's watch close to his heart. Loneliness set in like the hunger of a lone, wounded wolf. It gnawed at his insides, and he thought his heart might carry that empty hunger for his mama and now for his dad to his death. He swallowed and stared at the glass with the carvings that had not been there before. What did they mean? Dad was the only one who could have carved them there. He knew Dad, but what did this mean? He clamped the watch closed and held it to his heart. "Dear Lord," he mouthed the words, "I need to know what my dad was trying to tell me, and without you, I have no earthly clue. Please! Show me. I need your help."

"What about those letters and numbers carved on the back of the watch? Could that be a clue?"

Clay jumped and whipped his head toward Beep. "What?"

"Look. On the back of the watch. There is something carved there, too."

He turned the watch over and blinked. "That wasn't there before," he whispered in awe. The carving was shaky, but it clearly read: PS119:162.

Beep nodded. "Your dad must have thought you would know what that means."

"I do know what it means." He licked his lips. "Psalm 119:162 is a verse in the Bible."

Beep was excited, "Get your Bible, and we'll figure it out."

Clay sighed, "I can't. Sheriff Ary shoved my knapsack under his desk before he left."

Beep dropped her head in her hands and groaned, but she popped it back up with a smile. "Then, maybe we can work on what your dad carved on the face of his watch." Beep sat up straight.

Clay clicked the pocket watch open again, and together they huddled over it.

Clay bit his bottom lip and mumbled, "The arrow is going counterclockwise, and that has to mean something. Watches always run clockwise."

"Well, duh, where do you think the word counterclockwise comes from? Clocks!" the girl giggled.

Clay glared, but only a moment before he joined her in laughter. When they calmed down, he ran his thumb over the edge of the watch. "Look. The knob that winds the watch hands is gone. Dad may have lost it, but I think he took it off on purpose. It must be a clue."

Beep grabbed his wrist. "Maybe he did that so the hands on the watch would stay where he placed them. That has got to mean something."

"Maybe." Clay studied the time. "That would make it twenty seconds after six fifteen." Clay could not concentrate. He shook his head. He should understand what his dad was trying to tell him. His dad had worked out puzzles with him many times, and they had created puzzles together, but this made no sense. Still, he stared at the watch.

Beep looked at him and decided to leave him to his thoughts. She reached over and caressed the dangling boot hanging from the other end of the watch chain. It was a delicate carving. The sides of the boot had cactus arms spread wide, sculpted to look like they were stitched into leather. The sole of the boot was smooth to the touch, but her favorite was the spur. The rowel rolled with ease on the base. She twirled it several times before she noticed something else. She pulled the boot closer. There was a hinge between the heel and body of the boot. Very gently, she slipped her fingernail between the sole and the boot. She pried. The third time, she put a bit more pressure into the prying, and the sole of the boot opened. A tiny pile of rocks spilt into her hand. She gasped, "Clay, look at this."

Clay sucked in his breath. "I didn't know there was a secret compartment."

Beep was wide-eyed. "These rocks were hidden in that boot." She opened her palm to display the hidden treasures. "And, look. This is the knob that winds the hands on the watch."

"Rocks?" Clay gasped. "Beep, those are not rocks. Those are diamonds."

"What? Diamonds? Real diamonds? How do you know they are real diamonds?" she asked.

"Look." He pulled her to the window and held one diamond between his fingertips to catch the light shining through the bars of their cell window. "They have to be diamonds. Look what they do in the light!"

The diamonds split the light rays from the window, causing dancing shards of colored light to splatter over the ceiling and rock wall.

Clay whistled. "Normal rocks, Beep, normal rocks are not going to do that. These have to be diamonds."

Beep's mouth hung open as she watched the light show. "Did you know your dad had diamonds?"

Clay shrugged. "I didn't even know the boot had a secret compartment."

"It gives me shivers," Beep glowed. "Diamonds. We have a handful of diamonds. I wonder what they are worth?"

Clay closed his hand over Beep's handful of diamonds and whispered. "They are worth murder, Beep. I'll bet that is why your papa and my dad and all the other men were killed. It had to be these diamonds."

"Murder?" Beep let the handful of diamonds fall into Clay's palm, which, like lightning, he poured back into the boot and clicked the lid shut.

"Diamonds?"

Clay and Beep whirled around to stare at 'Puty Sneedle.

"Diamonds? That is my treasure!" 'Puty Sneedle shouted, sprang from his cot, and blasted to the bars separating the two from him. With both hands, he grabbed a bar and wildly shook. "I want my diamonds, and you had better give them to me, or I'll kill you!" he roared like a bear awakened early from hibernation.

Clay and Beep backed as far away from the wall of iron bars as their cell would let them. They were glad to be locked in and glad 'Puty Sneedle was locked out.

"I sure wish the sheriff would come back," Beep whispered.

Clay nodded and whispered, "Greater is he that is in me than he that is in the world." He paused before he added, "At least 'Puty Sneedle is on the other side of the bars."

Beep's eyes were huge. "I wish 'Puty Sneedle was on the other side of the world!"

'Puty Sneedle had burst into a rage. He jumped at the bars, wildly climbing halfway up and yanking to pull the bars free from their sockets. He splattered horrible words covered with spit through the air."

"I really wish the sheriff would come back!" Beep choked.

"Then pray." Clay stepped in front of the girl to keep her safer.

"Jesus, we need you now!" And with that prayer, Beep dove beneath the cot.

"Lord God Almighty," Clay breathed as a bar loosened in 'Puty Sneedle's hand. "If that madman keeps going, he will be in our cell!"

Beep opened her eyes from her first prayer since her papa had passed, and found herself face to face with a hairy monster pressing its wet nose against hers. Its glowing eyes gave the surrounding darkness a green sheen. Beep screamed. She half-crawled and hurdled herself from beneath the cot. The cot leg tangled in her clothing, and Beep grabbed it desperately. She threw the cot as if it were an enemy, cutting through the air. The cot just missed Clay as he yelled and dove to the side.

Attached to the bottom of the cot was the hairy monster screaming a haunting wail that set the world on end.

'Puty Sneedle froze.

The hairy monster was a huge tabby cat who bristled its shaggy hair, bared its teeth, and raked its claws, skidding over the stone floor. The cat screeched and barreled through the jail bars. The monster cat dug its claws into the leg of 'Puty Sneedle, climbing up his legs and over his back to squat on his head.

'Puty Sneedle dropped from the bars and careened in circles, trying to get the beast pried from his head. He zipped around his jail cell, yelling ungodly words and making promises to God he would never keep. The cat dug its claws in deeper.

Clay and Beep stood as statues side-by-side in wonder, their hearts pounding like wind-up toys.

Jailhouse Picnic

Chapter #23

The front door crashed open, and Sheriff Ary stood with gun in hand. A look of disbelief crossed his face, and then humor sank in. A chuckle bubbled up and burst into a guffaw of belly laughter. Finally, as he wiped tears from his eyes, he called over his shoulder. "Come on in. It's safe, but you'll have to see this to believe it."

By now, 'Puty Sneedle was plastered against the back wall of his cell, breathing hard. His hair sprayed in every direction, and a dribble of blood ran down his forehead and followed the side of his nose, catching in his mustache. The big yellow striped cat sat on its haunches in the middle of the cell, twitching its tail while glaring at 'Puty Sneedle.

Sheriff Ary walked toward the cell. "I see you met my mouser, Maude."

"That cat? That cat must be from Hell itself!" 'Puty Sneedle spat.

Maude whipped her paw toward the man and hissed.

Sheriff Ary slowly nodded. "Could be. She sure could be, or maybe she has just swallowed all the hell she has scared out of all the prisoners I've had in my jail. She is rather like my deputy." He chuckled, "Deputy Maude. You and she should get along well, since you are both deputies. I leave her in charge when I need to step out of my office for a while. She does a mighty fine job. And when I don't have any borders, I take her to church with me on Sundays. She seems to enjoy the services."

'Puty Sneedle narrowed his eyes. "To church? That rabid cat? You must be plumb crazy."

Sheriff Ary laughed. "I think she has pretty good taste in people. Come on, Deputy Maude." He snapped his fingers.

Maude pranced back and forth in front of 'Puty Sneedle before she turned and moseyed through the bars and over to Sheriff Ary. She wound around his left leg, through his legs, and then around his right leg before she settled at his feet, mewing all the while.

"Good girl, Maude," he dipped down and scruffed her neck.

Deputy Maude purred in a deep contralto.

With a smile on her shiny face, Valina swayed into the office. "Now, Sheriff Ary, you best take a hold of that deputy you got there 'cause I done got food in the basket, and it taint for her." Her eyes narrowed a bit as she set them on the young kids in the jail cell. She pointed a finger at the sheriff. "Just why do you have my great niece locked up?"

"Aunt Valina?" Beep whispered. She reached over and grabbed Clay's arm. "Do you think that is my granny's sister?"

Clay shrugged. "Kinda looks like her in the face. It's just that your granny is tall and thin, and your aunt is short and…" He stopped, not knowing how to say what he thought.

Aunt Valina had no problem. She giggled and swayed toward the bars, "Fluffy. That's what Martin calls me. Soft and fluffy."

Clay was embarrassed, but he couldn't hold the laughter he felt.

Aunt Valina turned to the sheriff. "I'm waiting for an explanation, Sheriff. Why are these children behind bars? Why, I can't even hug my great niece."

Sheriff Ary slowly took his hat off and hung it on a peg. "Mrs. Valina, the deputy here," he waved toward 'Puty Sneedle, "Deputy Sneedle told me they were runaways. I did not want them to run away while I was collecting you. If I locked them in the cell, I knew they would be safe." He ended with a smile.

"Safe?" Beep marched to the cell door. "Your deputy cat, Mouser Maude, scared my heart right out of my body. I nearly died."

Clay grinned, "Sure scared her, alright. Beep is a little bit of nothin', but she's the one who threw that cot clear across this cell. If I hadn't ducked, I'd be a goner, too. This jail cell hasn't been the healthiest place to stay, and I am sure glad you got back when you did." He pointed to 'Puty Sneedle. "I thought we might be planning a funeral."

Puty Sneedle whipped about and pointed his finger, "You just wait 'til I get my hands on you, Kid. You just wait."

Sheriff Ary crossed to the cells, "That isn't going to happen on my watch. These two minors will be under my protective custody until I hear otherwise."

"Them?" 'Puty Sneedle growled, "Them is the reason I came to you. We both work for the law. They are runaways, and I have first dibs."

"First dibs? What kind of legal term do you call that?" Sheriff Ary dropped his eyebrows.

"Louisiana legal. You had better contact Sheriff Millstrup in Rocky Branch, Louisiana. He's the one who swore me into office, and he's the one who will have a say about these runaways."

I have sent him a telegram, but until I hear anything from him, you will not lay a hand on either one of them."

'Puty Sneedle narrowed his eyes, "I do what my boss tells me to do. Not you."

"Then, Deputy Sneedle, welcome to my cell. Feel free to call it home until I hear differently." Sheriff Ary walked to the cell holding the minors and unlocked it.

Beep was the first out, and she stepped into the arms of her Aunt Valina. She certainly was soft and fluffy, and she smelled of homemade bread. It reminded her of her own granny, and unwanted tears bubbled over the edge of her eyelids.

Clay stood behind and scuffed his toe on the floor. It made him miss his mom and his dad. His heart was vacant, and he had to look away.

Aunt Valina let go of Beep and asked, "Your granny told me she had adopted a grandson, and he would be with you. Is this nice-looking young man him?"

Clay felt the fire burn his cheeks red.

Beep giggled. "It sure is, Aunt Valina."

Slowly, Aunt Valina stepped to the young man, pulled him close, and held him tight. "Welcome to our family, and I brought sandwich makings. Anyone interested?"

Clay was hungry for food, but even more, he was hungry for the touch of someone like Mom. She was fluffy, and she smelled like home. He hadn't been home for so long. He didn't dare to even breathe for fear the well pipe would reach the depths of his heart and water would gush out of his eyes.

Beep came to his rescue. "His name is Clay, and he is always hungry. I don't even know if he chews."

Aunt Valina stepped back and laughed. "Sheriff, I'm making a table of your desk. She crossed and set her basket right in the middle of Sheriff Ary's papers.

"As long as I get a sandwich, Mrs. Valina, you can set your basket anywhere you want. Just let me move my papers." He scooped up the pile and deposited it on a file cabinet in the corner.

It was then that a girl in striped overalls stepped up to help Mrs. Valina make sandwiches. She had sandy-colored hair and freckles scattered across her nose. She was taller than Beep and shorter than Clay.

Aunt Valina introduced her. "This is Maggie. She lives at the Gatlin Fields Mansion, and she has been working with me today. She is the best help, so I brought her along. Maggie, this is my niece, Bee Poppy, and my nephew, Clay."

Maggie's smile was warm and inviting. In no time, the two girls were friends, and the sandwiches were made.

Aunt Valina asked Sheriff Ary to pray.

"Yes, Ma'am." He bowed and thanked the God above for the blessings below, especially that of Mrs. Valina's food.

The kids gathered on the floor in the furthest corner away from 'Puty Sneedle. Even 'Puty Sneedle got a sandwich with Aunt Valina's warning, "Chew carefully. Sometimes sandwiches choke the ungodly."

Clay's eyes popped wide.

Beep dropped her mouth open, "That is something my granny would say."

Clay swallowed, "She is your Granny's sister."

Maggie laughed. "Bee Poppy, Mrs. Valina always says what's on her mind, no matter who's around."

Clay bumped into the conversation, "Maggie, I call her Beep." He nodded toward the girl.

"Beep? Why?" Maggie asked.

"She's like one of those car horns. She makes noise wherever she goes and tries to push things out of her way," Clay smiled.

Maggie laughed, "Good for you, Beep. We'll be good friends."

Clay rolled his eyes and took another bite of his sandwich. "Girls! Great! Now there are two of them?"

Sheriff Ary had pulled up a chair for Mrs. Valina, and they sat at the desk. Deputy Maude whisked through his legs and purred, begging for food. Sheriff Ary pulled a chunk of ham and dropped it for her with a warning. "But, Maude, that is the last you get. You've already had half of my sandwich."

Maude seemed to understand what he said. She licked her chops and headed for the jail cell where 'Puty Sneedle sat on his cot, hurriedly devouring his sandwich.

Maude swished right through the bars, sat in front of him, and growled like a lioness.

'Puty Sneedle jumped on his cot and threw the whole of what was left of his sandwich at the cat. "Hope yer satisfied, you stinking, mangy critter. If I had my gun, I'd put you out of my misery!"

Sheriff Ary laughed, "You are spending tonight with Deputy Maude, so you might be careful what you say. You don't want to hurt her feelings."

'Puty Sneedle glared at the cat.

The sandwiches were delicious, but the little pastries filled with chocolate pudding were to die for.

'Puty Sneedle did get one and shoved the whole thing in his mouth before Deputy Maude could make a claim.

Beep beamed. "Aunt Velina, they are just like what my granny makes."

Valina smiled, "Your granny and I used to make them together all the time. I sure do miss her."

The Mansion

Chapter #24

"Now, Deputy Sneedle, I am driving this crew out to the Gatlin Mansion, but I am not leaving you alone. My mouser, Deputy Maude, will keep you company. You might want to take time to get to know each other," Sheriff Ary winked and snugged his hat on his head.

Clay stepped to the sheriff's desk and ducked beneath to retrieve his knapsack. He wanted his dad's Bible and hoped it would answer the clue on the back of the pocket watch: PS119:162.

All five piled into the auto. Sheriff Ary drove with Aunt Valina beside him. The three kids were tucked in the back seat. It was crowded, but they didn't care.

"You live in a mansion with your mom and dad?" Beep asked.

Maggie blinked.

Beep shrugged. "Sheriff Ary said we were going to the Gatlin Mansion. I thought that meant you lived there."

Maggie narrowed her eyes and smiled, "Yes, I do."

"It must be wonderful to live in a mansion."

Maggie giggled, "We used to live in a boxcar."

"A boxcar?"

"Yep."

"That had to be a tight fit," Beep's eyes were wide.

"It was, but it didn't take long to clean," Maggie grinned.

Beep shrugged. "I guess it wouldn't. But why? You moved from a boxcar into a mansion?"

Maggie nodded, "It is a long story. Sue was living in the boxcar when she married my daddy. My daddy is my real dad, but my mama, Sue, is one God gave me after my real mama died."

With wide eyes, Beep touched her arm. "I'm sorry. I know it is very hard to lose someone you love."

Maggie smiled, "It is, and I loved my mama with my whole heart, and I guess I always will. But God gave me another mama that is everything I need and want." She paused for a bit before she continued. "All of us kids at the Gatlin Mansion have lost someone we love, and Annabelle Leigh has lost both her mom, her dad, and her gramps."

Beep grimaced, "That is morbid."

Maggie's eyes glowed. "I guess it is to start with, but my daddy and my mama, Sue, have their hearts filled with God's love, and it just overflows. They love all of us, and now Annabelle Leigh is a member of our family. We love her, and she loves us."

Clay had been sitting quietly, but he had heard every word. "Just how many of 'us' are there?"

"Right now? There are eight. With both of you there will be ten."

Clay narrowed his eyes. "And how big is this mansion?"

Maggie laughed, "It's the biggest place I have ever been in. Even with ten kids, there will be plenty of room to spare."

Beep leaned forward and touched Aunt Valina's shoulder. "I thought I was going to be staying with you."

Valina smiled, "Missy, you are welcome to stay with me if you choose. Martin and I only have one bedroom and an outhouse path out back. Maggie's dad has talked about adding a privy to our house, and I can't wait. This old age of mine would dearly love a privy. But right now, it is still the moonlight path. Now there are plenty of rooms at the Gatlin Mansion, and there are five big bedrooms on the second floor. And," she held her finger in the air, "there is a privy on each floor."

"Except the basement," Maggie giggled as she threw it into the conversation.

"Five big bedrooms, and a privy on each floor?" Clay furrowed his brows. "That sounds dangerous and scary."

Maggie laughed, "Actually, it is fun. And," Maggie looked him in the eye, "we, the girls, have two bedrooms, and you boys have two bedrooms. All the bedrooms are very big. Just wait until you see it."

"How many boys do I have to share with?" Clay asked.

"There are four. You will make five."

Clay spoke quietly, "Is this some kind of an orphanage or a workhouse? Because if it is, tell them to stop the auto. I want out."

"A workhouse?" Beep gasped.

Aunt Valina turned to look at her niece over the back of the seat. "No, ma'am, it is not a workhouse. Don't you fret. Maggie's new mama and her daddy own and run the place. It is a home full of the love of God."

A quiet settled over the auto.

Maggie smiled, "It is a home, and I love it. None of the boys can really be called an orphan. Cecil and Elbert are brothers, and they tend to get into trouble all the time. Their mom is bedfast, and their father had to work, so he sent them to live with their aunt and uncle. But their Aunt Louise got shot, and she needed help, so we have the boys until she gets better…if she ever does."

Aunt Valina chuckled. "She will take her sweet time, but it is a good place for those boys until then."

Maggie giggled. "It sure is, and I think Cecil and Elbert like living with us. Jed and Jess like it, too. They lost their mother four or five years ago, and their father is in prison, hopefully for a long time. Jed and Cecil are close to your age, Clay. Elbert and Jess are a few years younger."

"You promise it is not a workhouse?"

Maggie tipped her head and smiled. "Promise, cross my heart and hope to die," she whispered and very carefully slid her finger across her throat as she had seen Clay do.

Clay grinned.

"You will have chores, but chores are healthy. They teach us responsibility."

"Wow!" Beep dropped her mouth open, grabbed the back of the front seat, and rested her chin on it. "Look at that!"

A man swung open the gate, and Sheriff Ary slowed. "Howdy, Martin. Good to see you again."

"Yes, Sir, Sheriff. Good to see you, too." Martin touched his forefinger to his head.

"Martin, Martin!" Valina called across the front seat and out the window. "This is our great niece, Bee Poppy!"

Martin grinned, "I can sure tell. She looks just like you and your sister, Ouida, when y'all were little girls."

Valina beamed, "She's wonderful."

"She sure is," he winked. "Beautiful, just like her granny and Aunt Valina."

Beep's heart skipped a beat as she sucked in her breath. "That man looks like my papa!"

Gently, Valina turned. "He should look like your papa. They were brothers. Didn't your granny tell you?"

Beep shook her head. She could not hold back the tears.

"Oh, Honey, Honey, my dear, sweet child," Valina whispered. "I'm sorry. My sister probably didn't know how to tell you, and maybe she just couldn't think about the matter right now."

"You mean that you and your sister married brothers?" Maggie asked.

"We sure did. It just felt natural and comforting. We thought we would be together forever, but the good Lord had different plans. Ouida and I haven't seen each other in years." Valina's eyes held longing magnified by a gathering of tears. Then she turned to the girl and patted her cheek. "But, praise the good Lord, I get to be with my great niece." She turned to wipe her tears.

Sheriff Ary pulled through the gate, and Martin stood for a quiet moment before he shut it after them.

At the front portico, they piled out of the auto. Maggie ran up the steps onto the porch and turned to motion them to follow. Beep took Aunt Valina's hand, but Clay stood with his pack, looking up the steps. If he passed through those doors, would it capture him? Would his past…his dad…be left behind? Would he be giving up all hope he had of his dad being alive?

Sheriff Ary shut the auto off, opened the door, and stood. He slipped the key into his pocket and stepped to stand beside the boy. "It is a place filled with good, Clay, good, God-fearing people. You can trust them."

Then he waved his hand toward the door. "Shall we step inside?"

Clay studied the enormous double doors standing wide in welcome. He could almost hear his dad whisper, "Son, it will be safe. It is in God's hands, and God never misplaces anyone who belongs to Him."

Family

Chapter #25

Finally. The grand tour of the mansion was long over. Supper was finished and put away. Quiet time with the gathering of 'family' as it was, was splendid. Tonight, the gathering was on the wide back porch.

In the quiet of the evening shadows, Maggie's daddy read, "Ephesians 3:14-21 'For this cause I bow my knees unto the Father of our Lord Jesus Christ, Of whom the whole family in heaven and earth is named, That he would grant you, according to the riches of his glory, to be strengthened with might by his Spirit in the inner man; That Christ may dwell in your hearts by faith; that ye, being rooted and grounded in love, May be able to comprehend with all saints what is the breadth, and length, and depth, and height; And to know the love of Christ, which passeth knowledge, that ye might be filled with all the fulness of God. Now unto him that is able to do exceeding abundantly above all that we ask or think, according to the power that worketh in us, Unto him be glory in the church by Christ Jesus throughout all ages, world without end. Amen.'"

Maggie's daddy closed his Bible, and with a smile touching his heart, he said, "Family. Everyone sitting on this porch is missing a hunk of their family. It digs a big hole in your heart not easily filled. Jesus Christ died on the cross to patch that hole…if you will let him.

It is easy to invite Him into your heart to begin the rebuild. My mama taught me this:

A. Ask. First, you must ask him to come into your heart because he is not a robber or a thief. He will not break in and steal your heart. He wants to be your invited guest…forever. And someday Jesus will return the favor. He will open the doors to Heaven and invite you in…forever.

B. Believe. The next thing my mama told me was: You must also believe Jesus is the Son of God and believe he is without sin. He took your sin on that cross with him that he might die in your place. Yet he did not stay dead. He rose on the third day to conquer death. Now he sits on the right hand of the Father in heaven.

C. Confess. You must confess that your sins were the nails that nailed him to the cross, where he shed every drop of his lifeblood for you. When you ask him to be your Saviour, you are adopted into his family…forever."

Stars lit and twinkled in the dusky sky. A cool breeze touched Clay's face, and he could feel wet tears escaping his eyes. He lifted his shirt tail and wiped them away. Maggie's daddy sounded so much like his own dad, and his heart ached. His eyes slipped over all sitting on the porch. Could he ever consider them family? He knew Jesus was in his heart even though he felt so alone and empty. Mom was gone, and he was getting used to that, but Dad? Was he gone, too? And could he ever get used to being alone?

"If you have Jesus in your heart, you will never be alone. And," Maggie's daddy held up his finger, "You are in my family just like the Holy Book says, "For this cause I bow my knees unto the Father of our lord Jesus Christ, of whom the whole family in heaven and earth is named."

"Family?" Clay whispered. Then he felt Beep scoot closer to him and wrap her hands about his arm.

Maggie's daddy smiled. "If Jesus lives in your heart, your new family name is 'Christian'. That name was passed down by the Christians in Antioch because those who had Jesus Christ in their hearts acted like Jesus Christ. The world meant it to make fun of the Christians, but the Christians latched onto the name as if it were a badge of honor."

Beep squeezed his arm and whispered, "Clay, is he a preacher like your dad was?"

Clay swallowed over the word 'was', then he shrugged. "It kind of sounds like it."

Maggie giggled, "No. My daddy is not a preacher. He is just a farmer, but he loves the Lord. I think he wants us to love the Lord, too."

Clay nodded, "He sounds just like my dad."

"He was a preacher?" Maggie asked.

Clay nodded. "I hope he still is."

Maggie narrowed her eyes. "What do you mean that you hope he still is?"

Clay looked far away through the evening shadows of dusk. "I haven't seen him in a long time. One of his friends, a co-worker, Arthur Kent, told me he had found him. Someone had tried to kill him, and he was hanging on for dear life. Mr. Kent couldn't move him, so he hid him where the enemies could not find him to finish their killing job." Clay tinkered with his dad's pocket watch before he pulled it out of his pocket. "My dad had Mr. Kent give me this in case he didn't make it."

Maggie glanced at the watch for a moment before she drilled her eyes into his. "Do you think this means your dad didn't feel like he was going to make it?"

Clay closed his hand about the watch and pulled it to his chest. He swallowed. "Pretty much. His dad gave it to him, and he always told me it would be mine when he passed off the scene."

"Clay," Beep whispered, "Maybe your dad gave it as a clue. Maybe he is not dead. Mr. Kent was going to try his best to get back and help him."

"What kind of clue could it be?" Maggie asked.

"Well…" Beep started.

Maggie's daddy interrupted, "Time for bed. Say your good nights and sleep well."

As everyone stood to head back into the house, Maggie clutched Clay's arm and whispered, "When everyone is asleep, meet me in the ballroom. Bring the watch."

Clay nodded.

Beep took Clay's other arm and glared. "Not without me. I am coming, too."

Maggie blinked. "Well, of course. I want you there, but not Opal and Ruby. Those two can't keep a secret, and they sure can't keep quiet. Annabelle Leigh can, and if she is awake, I may bring her, too. She is pretty good at figuring out secret messages."

Before they could step into the house, an auto horn shattered the peaceful night. Sheriff Ary swung around the corner of the mansion and slammed on the brakes. Dust poured over the auto, blanketing it in a thick cloud.

Sheriff Ary shut off the ignition, opened the door, stepped out of the auto, and slammed the door shut. "Mrs. Valina told me that you were gathered back here." Sheriff Ary whipped off his hat, whopped it on his leg a couple of times, and a dust cloud formed.

Maggie's daddy stepped forward. "Something wrong, Sheriff?"

Sheriff Ary sighed. "Yes, Daniel. I am afraid it is. Deputy Sneedle escaped."

Beep gasped and stepped closer to Clay.

"How? Did he have help?" Maggie's daddy asked.

"I don't think he had help. It looks as if he worked on one of the bars that separate the two cells until he got it loose enough to yank it out. Seems he was so skinny he could squeeze right through the two-bar space, and apparently, he walked right out the front door."

Sue turned to the children. "All of you, get inside now. Get ready for bed, and we will be by to check on you after we talk to Sheriff Ary."

"The sheriff rubbed his forehead. "I never dreamed he could escape in such a short time, and not by yanking out a cell bar. Why I helped cement those bars in place. I am truly sorry, and I plan to stand guard all night right here with you, Daniel."

Maggie's daddy nodded, "Paul, it was not your fault. But, I would be glad for your company tonight."

"Oh," the sheriff held his finger in the air. "I brought reinforcements." He walked to the trunk and opened it. Deputy Maude shot out of the trunk and flew up the porch steps, screeching all the way. The kids dove in every direction. Sue ran inside the house, and Maggie's daddy kicked the fur ball without thinking. Maude soared through the air and landed on the roof of the auto.

By that time, Sheriff Ary was on the porch, waving a cane-backed chair in his hand as if he were training a lion.

Deputy Maude stretched, pranced around the auto top, and screamed a warning to all in listening distance. Then she curled up, making her bed as if to sleep, but anyone near enough could see the glow of her yellow eyes from the slit she refused to close.

Dad's Pocket Watch

Chapter # 26

Clay lay in bed and breathed a breath of comfort. This was the softest bed he had ever slept in. He rolled to watch the moon out the window. He was glad for the cozy light, fingering the open western Kansas night sky. He grinned to himself. The night sky of Kansas was one of the things he had missed the most. The stars displayed themselves as if they were forever staging a night show, and the moon? Well, the moon's personality refused to settle on one face. She was forever blushing as a sliver, or her whole round face watched your every move. Sometimes she was only half there, looking back on the day that had passed and toward the darkness to come. And…sometimes she found a sky-nook and slept, letting full dark have its way over the night.

Clay smiled. Not often did he see the full night sky in Louisiana. The trees crowded the view, and fog quilted the land. Maybe that was why the frogs wailed the night away. They were begging to be free of the dark cover of thick fog, which hid their enemies so well. Enemies. Clay shivered as he thought of the enemies. He had heard the cry of the black panther, but he had never seen it. Yet he was sure the black panther had seen him. Chills ran across his back with the memory. The deadly water moccasins dropped from trees without a sound, or they slithered through the water with only their heads above for a warning. At least in Kansas, the diamond-backed rattler shook his booty to a dance tune you knew, and you could accept him as a battle partner or turn and run.

Clay smiled. What a difference in this big country of America. He looked about the room. Everyone seemed to be asleep, so now was as good a time as any. Without a sound, he slipped from the cozy bed to stand barefoot on the floor. He had set out his dad's Bible on the bedside table, and he had stuffed the pocket watch into his trouser pocket. Quickly, he whisked them on, pulled off the night shirt, and replaced it with his everyday shirt. He grabbed up his boots and padded to the door on his bare feet.

Holding his breath, he moved through the hall to the stairs. It was only one flight up to the ballroom, and he was glad. He knew Maggie and Beep would be coming, but he wanted to be the first there. At the top of the stairway, he took a deep breath and stepped through the ballroom doors. He stopped in wonder. It was beautiful. Moonlight filtered through the big stained-glass window and shone in pastel hues across the waxed wooden floor.

It was like being in a grand church on Sunday morning before everyone else got there. He grinned. He had only been in a church like that once in Baton Rouge, Louisiana. Dad had taken him before any services had started. They were the only ones in the building. The quiet was overwhelming, and the stained glass in the sunrise was splendid. He would never forget that moment. He had wished his mom could have seen it, but when he told his dad, his dad had smiled. "Son, your mom is looking down from the other side of the stained glass of Heaven. I imagine what she sees is indescribable. She probably can't wait for you to share it with her."

Mom. What a warm, lonely spot in his heart she was.

The girls would be here soon, but Clay pulled out the pocket watch and looked at the verse etched into the back. He should know this verse, but he wanted to be sure. If it were a clue, it would have to be word-perfect. He took his dad's Bible and turned there. Silently, he read the words. He read them three times and finally whispered them out loud. "I rejoice at thy word, as one that findeth great spoil.'"

His heart beat a little faster. It surprised him how much one verse of the Bible could make his dad seem so close. He heard something. Chills spread across his body while he searched the room. He swallowed as he swerved about on his backside to check behind. Nothing lurked in the shadows.

A tinkle of a giggle sounded at the door. Clay let out the breath he had been holding. The girls. It must be impossible for them to be quiet.

Maggie stepped through the door and leaned against the wall. Beep swept in and stopped. She gasped in awe. She inched closer to the shimmering light and whispered, "This feels like Jesus is right here with us." She shivered and gracefully eased to the floor beside Clay.

Clay tenderly nodded. "Beep, I knew you still believed, and I knew God would show Himself to you."

"But my papa is dead, and I am here. That is not how I wanted my prayers answered."

Silently, Maggie eased to Beep's side, sat, and took her hand.

"Beep," Clay began, "God doesn't answer the way you tell Him to. God answers in the best way for you. He made you, and He knows what is best for you."

"Then what about my granny? You cannot tell me Papa's death was best for her."

"Are you smart enough to tell God it is not? Or are you telling God he made a mistake?" Clay's voice was gentle, but it carried the heavy hammer of truth.

Beep closed her eyes. "No. I won't tell God that, but it is so hard, and I just plain don't understand."

Maggie whispered, "My mom, Sue, told me I may not understand the whys of God this side of heaven. She said I was to let Jesus keep my heart in his hands, and someday, whether here or there, Jesus would reveal the whys to me. I just need to let him hold my heart until someday."

Tears slipped over her cheeks and caught the pastel colors lit by the full moonlight from the stained-glass window.

Clay could only think of what a rich bottle of tears Beep would have waiting for her in heaven.

Hiding his face, he swiped his shirt sleeve over his own cheeks.

Softly, Maggie whispered, "Dear Jesus, touch and heal Beep's heart and Clay's heart, and open our thoughts to the mystery you have placed in Clay's hands, and thank you for your help, Lord of all the earth."

As eyes opened, they settled on Clay. In a hushed voice, Beep asked the question. "Did you figure out what the verse said etched into the back of your dad's pocket watch?"

He laid the Bible down in the middle of the circle and read the verse out loud. "I rejoice at thy word, as one that findeth great spoil." He looked at each in the circle. "Any ideas?"

Maggie was smiling.

Beep was bouncing.

Clay grinned. "Both of you know?"

Maggie nodded.

Beep busted forth, "My papa always talked of riverboat pirates. They sailed up and down the rivers from the Gulf of Mexico after they had plundered ships on the seas. The pirates called their stolen treasures 'spoil'. Spoil means treasure!" She couldn't help herself; she clapped her hands and giggled. "Treasure!"

Maggie laid her hand on the Bible. "God's Word is full of great treasure!"

Clay was beaming. "Yes, it is, and that is the message Dad is sending us. He has the treasure hidden somewhere, and the clues are written on this watch and hidden in his Bible." Gently, he scooped up his dad's Bible. He flipped through it and found nothing. He held it upside-down by the spine and fanned through the pages, but nothing fell out. He pulled the book to his chest, looked to the ceiling, and whispered, "Lord, I know my dad is trying to pass something important to me, but I need your help."

Beep spoke softly. "Remember the carved boot? Those diamonds have got to be a part of the treasure."

"Diamonds?" Maggie's voice lightly touched the air.

"Show them to her," Beep nodded toward the pocket watch cradled in his pocket.

In the solitude, Clay took out his dad's watch. Tenderly, he held the carved boot in his left hand, and with his right hand, he pinched the spur and rolled it into position. Then he pried the sole of the boot open and poured the contents into Beep's palm. Each stone caught the pastel light, throwing brilliant, dancing rays.

Maggie gasped, "Are those real?"

"They must be. They are treasure," Beep grinned.

Clay licked his lips. "I think they are only part of a treasure. We have only figured out this much, but there must be more."

"More?" Maggie asked.

"Where?" Beep's voice rose.

Maggie pressed her forefinger to her lips and blew air through them as a warning.

Beep nodded and looked over her shoulder toward the steps coming into the ballroom. She eased out a relieved sigh. No one was rushing up the stairs. No one had heard. They were safe. She pulled her eyes back to Clay's and mouthed her question, "What is the next clue?"

Carefully, he took the handful of diamonds from Beep and placed them back in the boot. He snapped the sole shut and spun the spur, locking it in place. Then he took the pocket watch and flipped it open. "Look at this arrow scratched into the glass. Do you notice anything out of place?"

Both girls studied the watch. Beep shook her head, but Maggie tipped her head to one side and squinted her eyes.

"You notice something, Maggie?" Clay asked.

She hesitated. "I don't know if it could mean anything or not."

"What?" Beep asked.

"Well, I noticed something contrary to a watch. The arrow is etched counterclockwise, but the hands on a watch always move clockwise. I don't know if that could be a clue?" Maggie raised her eyebrows.

Clay grinned. "That is what I thought, too. Knowing my dad, it has to be a clue. The watch hands have got to be a clue, too, because Dad made sure they were stopped at special places. He took off the knob on the winding stem so the hands could not be moved."

"That's why the knob is gone. Gone on purpose for the protection of the clue!" Beep whistled.

With a smile, Maggie took a piece of paper and a pencil from her pocket. "I thought we might need these."

"That was good thinking," Clay smiled. "Let's write down the hands and the numbers they are stuck on to see if that means anything."

Maggie nodded with a poised pencil.

Clay started. "The hour hand is on six. The minute hand is on fifteen, and the second hand is on twenty."

Maggie wrote it down and read, "Six, fifteen, twenty?… Twenty seconds past 6:15?"

"What does that mean?" Beep wanted to know.

Maggie shook her head while Clay studied the paper. "I don't think it has to do with time. I know my dad. It has got to mean something else."

Beep pressed her lips together in thought before she spoke. "Clay, it has three numbers. Could that be some kind of location?"

Clay squinted his eyes in thought. "Longitude. Latitude." He shrugged his shoulders, "Altitude?"

Both girls giggled.

"Well, maybe," Beep said, but her words carried doubt.

Maggie sighed. "We know there are three numbers. Think of something that needs three numbers."

Beep tipped her head, "Combinations usually have three numbers. Does your dad have a lock box somewhere?"

Clay frowned, "I don't think so, but my dad seems to have lots of secrets which I know nothing about."

"Clay," Maggie's thoughts were tumbling. "What is something that is important to your dad?"

Beep burst in, "Birthdays have three numbers! Month, day, and year. Could it be someone's birthday?"

Clay mumbled the numbers. Month. The only month it could be… would be June, because there is no 15th or 20th month. The only family birthday in June that I know of is mine. June first, but the first is not one of the numbers."

"What about your mom and dad's anniversary?" Maggie asked.

"January 14? Those numbers won't fit either." Clay sighed.

Maggie did not give up. "Think very hard, Clay. How were numbers important to your dad?"

Clay rubbed his hands over his face and through his hair. He looked at the pocket watch resting on his dad's Bible. Light sparked in his eyes. "Verses! Verses are always book, chapter, and verse!"

Maggie grabbed the paper and read the numbers. "Six, fifteen, twenty."

Clay pulled his dad's bible close and sped through the pages. "Six. The sixth book of the Bible is Joshua. That would make it Joshua chapter 15 verse 20." He ran his finger down the page and read: "'This is the inheritance of the tribe of the children of Judah according to their families.'"

Silence shrouded the group.

Beep was the first to ask, "Are you in the tribe of Judah?"

Clay shook his head, "No."

Maggie giggled, "That clue is really disguised. Clay, do you have any idea what it means?"

He dropped his chin in his hands, "No."

Both the girls watched him.

Suddenly, he grabbed his dad's pocket watch and stared. "That's it! We left out this part!" He traced his finger over the arrow shooting counterclockwise. "Counterclockwise! What are the numbers counterclockwise?"

Maggie yanked the paper back to her. "Backwards? Twenty, fifteen, six."

Like a whirlwind, Clay yanked the Bible to him and began counting to the twentieth book of the Bible. "Proverbs! What's the next number?"

"Fifteen." Maggie answered.

Clay flipped the pages. "Proverb chapter 15. And the last number?"

"Six!"

His finger landed on verse six, and he read, "'In the house of the righteous is much treasure: but in the revenues of the wicked is trouble.'"

Both girls leaned in. "What does it mean?"

"Give me a minute," Clay whispered. He read the verse again, licked his lips, closed his eyes, and recited the verse. The boy laughed.

"Clay?" Beep nudged into his laughter. "What is funny?"

His face was aglow. "That verse is one of the first verses my dad had me memorize. He taught me what it meant by preaching it and living it."

"Does that mean you know where the treasure is?" both girls wanted to know.

"You bet it does. I know exactly where the treasure is!"

"Good!" The hammer of a revolver clicked, ripping through the excitement and killing the joy. Hearts were racing as all eyes shot toward 'Puty Sneedle.

A Shot in the Night

The Secret Will Die With Me

Chapter #27

'Puty Sneedle's face bore the marks of Deputy Maude, Sheriff Ary's mouser: the monster cat. It made him look like the walking dead. His hair was matted on one side with a few patches sprouting from his head as a growth of thick, mangy moss. One eye was almost swollen shut, but he strained to hold it open as wide as he could. The other eye almost popped from the socket as it roved over the ballroom. His shirt was ripped, exposing chunks of wadded-up hair. He had pinned the rip together with the only thing he had…his badge, and it was upside-down. He stood, legs apart to steady himself, and gun pointed. "Kid, I want that watch, and I want it now!" He growled.

"No, Sir," Clay spoke boldly. "It is my dad's watch, and he meant for me to have it."

"I don't care what your pa meant, Kid. He ain't here. He's dead. I killed him, and I know that watch has part of my treasure stuffed in that boot hooked to it. And it's a clue to where the rest of my treasure is hidden. So, I want that watch, I need that watch, and Kid, you are going to give it to me!" 'Puty Sneedle bared his teeth as a mad dog. "And, Kid, I will shoot you if need be." He swung his gun in the air.

Clay blinked. "It won't do you no good. I am the only one who understands my dad's clues. You kill me, and the secret will die with me!" Clay shoved the watch deep in his pocket.

'Puty Sneedle chuckled, "That the way of it then, Kid?"

Clay nodded. "That is how it works."

The shaky 'Puty Sneedle whipped his gun toward the girls. "Get over here, the both of you."

Maggie gasped and backed up a step.

Beep clenched her fists and, with her eyes wild and lit with fire, she ran toward 'Puty Sneedle. A war yell exploded from the petite girl as she torpedoed across the ballroom. "You killed my papa, and you tried to kill me! Murderer! Murderer!"

The pastel colors of the ballroom danced.

In shock, 'Puty Sneedle backtracked, tripping over his own feet. He hit the floor hard on his backside. His gun flew across the polished floor and spun in a circle. 'Puty Sneedle rolled over and frantically crawled across the floor toward his spinning gun.

Clay beat him to it. He snatched up the gun and aimed it at the deputy. Over his shoulder, he called, "Maggie, you got something to tie his hands and feet?"

"Yes, I do." She grabbed a gold cord that held back a ballroom curtain. "I'm coming."

But Beep was coming faster. She dove on the man, pounding his chest. Over and over she cried,

"You killed my papa! You murderer! You blasted murderer!"

'Puty Sneedle grabbed her hands in a death grip and pulled her face to his. "Your papa was going to take my treasure! I had to kill him!" he snarled through clenched teeth.

Beep tried to pull away and pry her hands from his big, grubby ones, but when she couldn't, her eyes lit with fire. She dropped to his shoulder and dug her teeth into his skin and yanked.

"Yeeeow!" he yelled. He let go of the girl and tried to toss her far away from him.

Clay pulled Beep from the man on the ballroom floor and dragged her away from his clutches. "'Puty Sneedle is dangerous, Beep. Remember that. Stay away from him!"

The girl was breathing hard and shaking like a cottonwood leaf in a whirlwind. She sputtered and spat to clear the taste of the horrible man from her mouth.

'Puty Sneedle scooted away and rattled through clenched teeth. "They all were trying to steal my treasure, and I had to stop them."

"Just how many men did you kill?" Clay asked.

'Puty Sneedle shrugged his shoulders, "Ten, maybe twelve, but I had orders. I had papers with names Sheriff Millstrup hid in a tree. He told me to take care of them all. They were trying to steal our treasure."

"What treasure?"

'Puty Sneedle's eyes were wild as he searched every corner of the ballroom. "The Confederate stash. The pipeline workers were looking for it, and I knew it wouldn't be long before they found it. They were bound to find it. And someone did find it. Someone took it! They took it, and they hid it!" 'Puty Sneedle narrowed his eyes as would a rattler. He stretched forth his arm and pointed at Clay, "It was that preacher man who stole it! I know it was him!"

"My dad?" Clay asked.

"The preacher man!" He turned and spat on the ballroom floor.

Marked steps clicked across the floor. Above him, Sue stood with her hands on her hips and her foot tapping. "You will not spit on my floor!" The words were quietly spoken, but abruptly articulated.

'Puty Sneedle blinked. "Yes, Ma'am." Slowly, he reached over and wiped it up with the torn sleeve of his shirt.

Maggie dropped the cord to the ballroom curtain beside the man. "You can use this to tie him up, Clay."

"Thanks, Maggie." As Clay turned to look at the girl, he noticed Maggie's dad, Sheriff Ary, and U.S. Marshal Arthur Kent." He gasped, "U.S. Marshal Kent! What are you doing here?"

The three men walked over to surround the man heaped on the floor.

That was when Ole Honker shoved over the top step, skidded across the polished floor, and, sliding to a halt by 'Puty Sneedle, pounced on the man sprawled on his back. With a growl, the hound's gaping mouth snapped on 'Puty Sneedle's neck, and the deputy screeched and froze.

"Ole Honker?" Clay dropped and hugged the growling chunk of his dog. "Good Ole Boy!"

"Get this rabid animal off me," 'Puty Sneedle gurgled.

"Stay," Clay patted his dog and looked up to U.S. Marshal Kent. "What are you doing here?"

Marshal Kent smiled. "I needed to check up on you and Beep, but mostly I followed 'Puty Sneedle. When he was gone, I figured he had headed out after you, and I knew he would be up to no good. I guess I figured it right." He pulled his handcuffs from his back belt and clicked them on the man, still frozen on the floor. Marshal Kent stood over the cuffed man and narrowed his eyes. "My Soul! I don't know what you ran into, Sneedle, but you look half dead." He wrinkled his nose, "You smell like it, too."

Maggie, Beep, and Clay laughed. Together they said, "He ran into Deputy Maude, Sheriff Ary's mouser."

"What kind of animal is that?"

"Just a cat," Sheriff Ary laughed.

Ole Honker's ears pricked at the word cat. He backed off the man and sniffed the air.

'Puty Sneedle coughed, "That beast can't be just a cat! I hope that beast and that dog meet. They will kill each other! I'd bet on it." 'Puty Sneedle started to spit again, looked up at Sue, and thought better of it. He swallowed the wad and choked.

U.S. Deputy Marshal Kent shoved his hat back on his head and squatted beside the prisoner. "You know, Sneedle, you are going to hang along with Sheriff Millstrup."

"For what?" he glared.

Marshal Kent chuckled, "For what? Sneedle, we were listening at the door while these kids got a confession out of you. From your own lips, you said you had killed ten to twelve pipeline workers. You hung yourself."

"Prove it! You ain't got no bodies!" A glare shot from 'Puty Sneedle's one good eye.

Quietly, Beep stepped forward and looked down with disgust at the man. "But, 'Puty Sneedle," she crossed her arms, "they have an eyewitness."

"Eyewitness? You? A girl? A shrimp of a girl? Ain't nobody going to hold store by that. Besides, who would believe the kind of girl who wanders out in the middle of the night!" The man laughed.

"I would." Clay stepped to her side. "I watched you fight with a dead man. I watched you shoot at Beep and me and my dog!"

"Another kid!" 'Puty Sneedle turned to look at the U.S. Marshal. "You can't convict me on the testimony of kids. You ain't got nothin'!"

Marshal Kent stood and smiled widely. "Sneedle, you can swing to your grave thinking that. These two are eyewitnesses, and we will put them on the stand…unless…unless you want to save them some trouble and plead 'guilty'."

'Puty Sneedle smashed his lips together in silence and glared.

U.S. Marshal Kent squatted again beside the man, letting his big hands dangle over his knees. "Sneedle, did you ever find the treasure, if there ever was one?"

'Puty Sneedle's wandering eye searched out Clay and landed on him. "That kid," he nodded toward Clay, "that kid knows where the treasure is. Let me out of these cuffs, give me a few minutes alone with him, and I'll tell you where that treasure is!"

Marshal Kent smiled. "That is not going to happen." He stood and walked a couple of steps closer to Clay. "Is 'Puty Sneedle right? Do you know where the treasure is?"

Clay swallowed. He was sure Marshal Kent was a good man, but what if the treasure was too much for him to stay on the good side of the law? What if the temptation was too great?

Marshal Kent smiled. "Your dad told me you would figure out the clues, and that you would walk me through them step by step so we could recover the treasure and get it to the rightful owners. He told me I could trust you. I guess the problem seems to be, can you trust me?"

Clay studied U.S. Marshal Kent's eyes. He licked his lips and finally spoke. "If my dad trusted you, I can trust you. If you lie, I will let God take care of you."

Marshal Kent nodded. "God be our judge." He reached out his hand for a handshake.

Clay took it, pumping it like a well handle.

"Let's start with your dad's broken pocket watch," Marshal Kent grinned. "I studied it plenty before I handed it over to you in the restaurant. I swear, I could not make heads nor tails of it."

Clay laughed, nodded, and pulled the watch from his pocket. "Dad has taught me all my life to read his sign, so I pretty well know where he is thinking. But Maggie and Beep helped with this code. I was thankful for their ideas." He laid the watch in his hand upside-down. "See this?" he tapped the back of the watch.

Marshal Kent nodded.

Quiet settled over the ballroom as everyone listened.

"PS119:162 is a verse."

Marshal Kent bumped the palm of his hand to his forehead, "I should have known! I thought it was coordinates, and I could not get them to make any sense at all!"

Clay grinned. "My dad taught me to listen to him. Now, the verse, etched on the back, is Psalm 119:162. I was pretty sure I knew the verse, but I wanted to be right, so I looked it up in Dad's Bible. It says, 'I rejoice at thy word, as one that findeth great spoil.' Spoil is treasure, so we figured we would find the treasure location somewhere in Dad's Bible."

"Did you?" Marshal Kent asked.

Maggie and Beep slipped beside Clay, their eyes glittering with excitement.

Clay smiled. He opened the watch to reveal the clue carved into its face glass by a sharp object. "This," he pointed to the arrow, "is carved counterclockwise. That is contrary to a watch, and my dad knew I would pick up on that clue. That meant Dad wanted me to follow the address to the verse in a backward order. See how he marked the numbers? Twenty seconds after six fifteen. The 20 is the twentieth book of the Bible, which is Proverbs. The minute hand points to chapter 15. And the hour hand is the verse number, making it verse number six. But if you said the time, it would be six fifteen and 20 seconds. See, it is counterclockwise or backwards." The boy looked into the Marshal's eyes.

Marshal Kent whistled. "In a hundred years, I would never have figured that out."

Maggie held Clay's dad's Bible out to him.

"Thanks, Maggie." He took the Bible and turned to Proverbs Chapter 15, verse six and read, 'In the house of the righteous is much treasure: but in the revenues of the wicked is trouble.'" Clay grinned.

Marshal Kent narrowed his eyes and studied the boy. "Does that tell you where the treasure is?"

"Yes, Sir, it sure does. I know right where this Confederate treasure is hidden."

"Well, where?" 'Puty Sneedle gaped at him. "Kid, that ain't no clue what makes any sense at all! You must be plumb local!"

Marshal Kent grinned. "I believe the boy. I don't have it figured out, and without his help, I doubt I ever would. But…I believe he knows exactly where this treasure is. Am I right, Clay?"

Clay nodded, "You sure are."

"Do you want to let us in on the secret?"

"I will, but I sure wish my dad were here."

Marshal Kent grinned, "I know you do, Boy. I know you do."

Clay took a deep breath and began. "'In the house of the righteous is much treasure.'" He paused before he explained. "The most righteous house I know is the Lord's house. Next, the end of the verse reads, 'In the revenues of the wicked is trouble.' The most wicked house I know is a brewery. If you think of Rocky Branch, you know that my dad held church services in the Branch Water Brewery Company, owned by Mr. Perry. Dad made a pulpit to use on Sundays while he preached to the people. All week it was kept in the back storeroom, but on Sunday mornings, Dad would have me go get that pulpit and set it in the spot he made for it. In fact, Dad marked that spot by carving an 'X' in the floorboards. Every Sunday, I set his pulpit on that 'X'." Clay's eyes sparkled. "I believe the treasure is under the floorboard that is marked with that 'X'."

Marshal Kent slapped his leg, "That has got to be where the treasure is!"

"AWE!" 'Puty Sneedle groaned. "Right in the middle of Rocky Branch. I never thought to look there," 'Puty Sneedle whined. "If I get loose from these cuffs…"

"That is not going to happen, Sneedle," Marshal Kent chuckled.

"But, if..,"

"No ifs about it, 'Puty. It won't happen." The Marshal crossed his arms.

"You better believe it won't happen, Sneedle!" a preaching voice boomed, and on crutches, Clay's dad hobbled into the ballroom, pastel lights dancing.

"Dad?" Clay swallowed a sob. "Dad! Dad! You are alive?"

Marshal Kent laughed. "You just bet your boots he's alive! He had too much to live for."

The boy rushed to his dad's side and wrapped his arms around him. "This is a dream come true…" Clay stopped and swallowed, "Really, it is a prayer come true. Dad, I missed you so much."

'Puty Sneedle shrieked. "A dream come true? It ain't no dream come true! It's a ghost! A walkin', talkin' ghost!" 'Puty Sneedle laid his eyes on Clay's dad and pointed a crooked finger, "You are dead, I know you are dead! I shot you, I hit you with the shovel, and I kicked you over the edge of Wilson Cave. I heard the splash! That's a fifty-foot drop! No one could live through that! He's got to be a ghost! Run for your lives and take me with you! Get me out of these cuffs and get me out of here!"

Again, the Marshal laughed, "Thank you for that confession, Sneedle." U.S. Marshal Kent waved his hand over all in the ballroom, "This whole audience can witness your confession and testify against you, which should shorten the trial. Would you like to pick out your own rope?"

'Puty Sneedle gasped as he shook. He glared and dropped his head, muttering things no one could understand about the living dead.

Marshal Kent grinned as he looked about the faces in the pastel light of the ballroom. "Only our God could have done this." He sighed as he studied the prisoner on the floor. "Let's get you back to Sheriff Ary's office. He has a cell waiting just for you."

'Puty Sneedle sneered, "That cell? It won't keep me long."

"It doesn't need to, Sneedle. You are headed back to the scene of your crimes for trial. There are a bunch of good people who want to see justice for their loved ones." Marshal Kent reached down and pulled his prisoner to his feet.

Beep was the first to notice the aroma wafting up the stairs. She sniffed the air and gasped, "What is that?"

Clay took a deep breath, "Beep, it smells like the Best Biscuits Around Café."

Beep shivered. She looked at Marshal Kent, "Marshal?"

The U.S. Marshal winked. "Your granny is very persuasive. She insisted on chaperoning me to Kansas." He waved his hands through the air. "Then your granny made me stop to wake up that sister of hers so they could fix an early breakfast for everyone."

"Granny? Granny's here?" Beep ran to the stairs and cascaded down.

Breakfast was wonderful, delicious, and early. The eggs were eaten before the rooster crowed!

All the adults sat around the huge table except for 'Puty Sneedle, whose ankle was tied to a heavy bureau leg, allowing him to use his cuffed hands to eat. The kids gathered on the floor opposite the deputy. Ruby and Opal watched him with wide eyes.

'Puty Sneedle glared at them, growled, and chuckled when they gasped, tore their eyes away from him, and giggled.

"Girls, it is not funny," Maggie scolded.

"No, it is not funny. He killed my papa," Beep whispered.

"You are right, Beep, it is not funny." Sheriff Ary glared at 'Puty Sneedle, who turned his eyes away from the girls.

Marshal Kent stood. "Ladies. Breakfast was great. Best Biscuits Around Café was always a busy place! But if you'll excuse us, we need to take care of Sneedle. Later, we will take statements, but get some rest if you can."

That was the last time Beep had to lay her eyes on the horrible man who killed her papa. She watched as the sheriff's auto drove 'Puty Sneedle away from the Gatlin Mansion. Nightmares would haunt her the rest of her life, but 'Puty Sneedle would pay for the murder of her papa.

Marshal Kent had explained, "I think the court will excuse Clay and Beep as they are underage, but we will need their statements.

Clay stood by his dad. It had been decided that the court could also use his statement rather than his presence because of his health, thereby avoiding another train ride. His dad shook hands with Marshal Kent, "If you need my testimony, I'll get there."

"I know you will, my friend. I know you will." Marshal Kent shook his friend's hand and hugged him before he stepped out the door.

Clay stood close to his dad. "Are you sure the court won't need us?"

His dad sighed, "Trial will start in three weeks, maybe a month. I'll be better then, and Son, if we need to or want to, we can go back to Rocky Branch. I'd kind of like helping the good guys win and watching the bad guys lose."

"Really?"

"Really." Dad pulled him into a hug. "Son, I am proud of you and the way you figured out my message to you."

Clay looked at his feet, then to his father, "You taught me, and you taught me to pray. I have never prayed like that before. I prayed every day that God would allow you to stay here and not take you to heaven. I miss mom so much, and I didn't want to have to miss you, too." Tears welled up in his eyes, and before they could overflow, he ran out the door and across the porch. He grabbed a porch pole, pressed his forehead to it, and held tightly. His tear jar in heaven must be running over. He choked back a sob, "Thank you, Lord God Almighty. Thank you for leaving me my dad."

From behind, a whisper stopped him. "But, He didn't leave me my papa."

Clay dropped his hands and turned to face Beep. "I am so sorry, Beep."

She swiped her hands over her wet cheeks. "It's okay, Clay. You were right. I know my papa was praying for anything to keep me safe from that horrible man, 'Puty Sneedle…even if it took his own life to save mine. I believe God answered my papa's prayer instead of mine."

Clay's dad stepped up to his son and the girl. He put an arm around them both. "What an honor that God Almighty takes His time to listen to us…and answer our prayers. Some answers bring joy, and some bring sorrow, but God always knows what is best for his children. Never quit talking to your heavenly Father."

The rooster crowed, and Clay felt the rumble in his tummy from eggs that the rooster was crowing about, and the Best Biscuits Around!

After the fact…

Newspapers across the country reported:

*Sheriff William Millstrup and his deputy, Irwin Sneedle were convicted of twelve counts of murder in the first degree. They were scheduled to hang by the neck until dead.

*The Confederate Stash was one of the biggest ever recovered. Out of the graciousness of their hearts, the people of Rocky Branch first agreed to provide a settlement for each family of the missing pipeline workers. With her settlement, Beep's Granny relocated to Dodge City, Kansas, and opened a restaurant she named: The Best Biscuits Around Café.

*For finding and keeping the Confederate Stash safe, Gregory D'Gregory, Clay's dad, was awarded the diamonds he had hidden in the carved boot on the end of his watch chain.

*Even though Beep and Clay were only thirteen, their hearts were knit together and sparks as the Fourth of July continued to shower about them, along with laughter and the love of God.